Miss Popularity

candy apple books...
just for you.
sweet. fresh. fun.
take a bite!

The Accidental Cheerleader
by Mimi McCoy

The Boy Next Door
by Laura Dower

Miss Popularity
by Francesco Sedita

How to Be a Girly Girl in Just Ten Days
by Lisa Papademetriou

Miss Popularity

FRANCESCO SEDITA

SCHOLASTIC INC.

New York Toronto London Auckland Sydney
Mexico City New Delhi Hong Kong Buenos Aires

ISBN-13: 978-0-545-00828-0
ISBN-10: 0-545-00828-X

Text design by Steve Scott
The text type was set in Bulmer.

12 11 10 9 8 7 8 9 10 11 12/0

Printed in the U.S.A.
First printing, January 2007

A List of Great People

Here's a list of super-tastic people: my mom and dad; Danielle; Mrs. June Davey, my 7th grade teacher; Ken; Craig, Catherine and Aimee; and Doug.

And, duh, like Sean. Sean.

CHAPTER 1

The Maine Event

Cassie Cyan Knight watched the hideous event unfold:

Erin Donaldson, Cassie's best friend since, well, ever, was in the midst of the most ungraceful spill in the history of Sam Houston Middle School's cafeteria. Her tray of food, including an uncapped Coke Zero, a plate of fried chicken and mac & cheese and an inexplicable quantity of napkins, literally flew in all directions as Erin herself went straight down.

Immediately, Cassie went into crisis mode. She put her tray down on the salad bar counter, took a deep breath, pushed her red tresses behind her ears, and locked her plastic teal bangle high on her arm so it wouldn't bang against her wristbone. Then she marched over to the scene. Kids were gawking and pointing at teary-eyed Erin. Cassie's troupe of girls, Jen, Marci, and Laura, followed in formation, each certain that she was the most important girl on the backup team. Every girl in Sam Houston — in the state of Texas, probably — wanted to be Cassie Knight's best friend.

Cassie waved the gaggle of giggling students off with a breezy, "Oh, come on, like you've never seen someone fall?" And then to a group of awed fifth graders, she added, "Guys, I mean, really? Move it. The show is over." She was firm but sweet. She was a Texan, after all. And Texas girls know how to strike that perfect balance.

Cassie leaned over and offered a trembling Erin her hand. Cassie would get her friend through this. They all would.

In a millisecond the girls — Cassie, Erin, Jen, Marci, and Laura — were in the Ladies Room, de-mac-&-cheesing, reglossing, and de-embarrassing their friend.

"Okay, young lady," Cassie said as she went through Erin's purse, extracting all the needed supplies: lip gloss, shimmery shadow, and, of course, hair spray. "Now it's time to either break down and cry or laugh. Either way, we have some work to do on that gorgeous face, so let me know."

Erin's face was blank. Cassie realized it was time to try a new tactic.

"Okay, so that was quite possibly one of the best falls I've ever seen!" Cassie said, wiping a glob of mac & chese from Erin's shoulder. Sooner or later, Erin was going to laugh. Cassie just wanted to get her there sooner. She made eyes at the other three girls, who were busy hair-spraying themselves in the mirror.

In unison, they said, "Totally!"

Cassie swooped the gloss wand across Erin's lips.

Erin sighed and crossed her arms. "Guys, please, people pointed and stared! Pointed, stared, and LAUGHED!"

Cassie caught her breath fast, hoping to hold back the fit of laughter about to slip out of her. She didn't want to laugh *at* Erin. But it *was* sort of hilarious.

Erin knew her too well. "Cassie Knight, I swear if you start laughing, I am going to add peroxide to your conditioner!"

Cassie put her hand on top of her head, guarding her red curls. "You wouldn't!" And with that, Cassie couldn't control herself and let laughter fly out of her. Through her gasps, she said, "I'm sorry,

Erin, it was so funny!" And then, "I had no idea Coke Zero could explode so much!"

The other girls lost it, too, squealing with laughter.

Erin was quiet for a minute. "Well, I *was* surprised to see mac & cheese could stick to the wall like that." She let out a slight giggle.

And then, the group howled together. Erin did, too, her hand in front of her mouth, her embarrassment slipping away.

"Okay, make me beautiful again," Erin said, pushing back her hair.

"That's our girl!" Cassie beamed, lining up the needed beauty supplies on the counter.

On the way home that afternoon, big Texas sunlight flooded the backseat of Mrs. Donaldson's minivan (the one with the bumper sticker that humiliated Erin: THE ONLY THING BIGGER THAN MY HAIR IS TEXAS). Cassie stretched her fingers apart, admiring the glint and glimmer of her favorite blue crystal ring and loathing the chip in her shimmering, shiny Blue by You nail polish. Blue — and if we're getting specific, teal — was Cassie's signature color. Oh, it was just so yummy! And it was the basis of Cassie's #1 Design Rule. *Teal: good. Teal and tons and tons of warm sunlight: um, delicious.*

"So, what are we doing this weekend?" Laura asked from the backseat.

Cassie turned around. "I heard that everyone's going roller skating on Saturday for Donny McMahill's birthday."

"Really?" Erin asked, dreamily. She'd had a total crush on Donny since second grade.

"We should go. And maybe hit the mall first?" Cassie asked.

All the girls nodded.

"Erin, what are you going to wear?" Cassie asked.

Erin went white. "I have NO idea!"

"We'll figure it out. We have plenty of time," Cassie said, confident. "You can borrow my new flouncy denim skirt if you want. It would look SO cute on you!"

"Really? Thanks!" Erin said. "Because, really, Coke Zero is *not* my color."

The girls started to laugh again. Cassie was relieved Erin could joke about her spill.

"What's going on back there?" Mrs. Donaldson asked, her eyes in the rearview mirror.

Cassie leaned forward and said, "It's nothing, Mrs. D. Your beautiful daughter had a relatively un-beautiful moment today. But we handled it. She's still as beautiful as ever, right?"

Mrs. Donaldson smiled. "Of course!" She lightly bounced her hand against her hair-sprayed head.

They turned past Palace Boot Shop, where Cassie got a new pair of cowboy boots each year for her birthday, and entered Houston Heights, Cassie's neighborhood.

Before she stepped out of the car, Cassie turned to the girls. "Okay, wrap-up calls in half an hour? Because we have some major homework to do. I can't believe it! It's like, welcome back from winter break, here's enough work to make you forget you had a vacation."

"Oh, please, Cass," Jen said, her copper-shadowed eyes twinkling in the sunlight, "you probably already did it all during free period."

Cassie grabbed her bag. "Thanks for the ride, Mrs. D!"

"Of course, sweetie. Tell your mom I'll call her later tonight."

"Will do!" Cassie looked at Erin, wanting to make sure her best friend was still okay after the unfortunate fall earlier. "How are we? Tell me before I go, so I don't have to start up CheerErinUp-dot-com when I get upstairs."

Erin laughed. "We are fine. Really. Thanks, Cass."

"It was funny. But so what? Funny is the best."

Erin smiled. Cassie reached over and gave her a hug.

Cassie blew kisses to the rest of the girls and slid out of the car, her teal blue Candies clicking on the cement. Feeling the slight chill of January in the Houston air, she walked through the yard toward her house, a reddish-brown brick beauty. Before Cassie crossed the lawn, she stopped to look at the big stone archway over the door. When she was a little girl, she used to imagine it was the entrance to her princess castle. Truthfully, she still did. She just wouldn't admit it to anyone!

"I'm home!" Cassie called, the heavy door sighing open. She dropped her backpack and ran upstairs to her room.

She put her purse down on her desk, next to her blue rhinestone laptop. Design Rule #11 was obvious — basic, really. *Glitter, sparkles, and marabou make a perfect accent to anything.*

Cassie sat carefully on her bed, making sure she didn't upset her perfectly arranged pillow pile. She reached for her cordless phone to call a few of her other girls, to report on a *fab* pair of wedge heels she'd seen at the mall. This was Design Rule #8: *The cordless (teal, of course, and not so easy to find!) must get killer reception, anywhere in the house.*

Cassie knew that might not technically be a Design Rule. But it was a rule. And it was important.

Just then, her mother called from downstairs. "Cassie, can you come to the kitchen, please?"

Cassie swung her feet onto the floor, slid on her marabou slippers, and walked to the mirror. She frowned at her frizzy mane, then sprayed hair spray with a flourish. Humidity in January was a real downer.

She clicked her fingernails against the banister as she walked down the stairs. She had to fix that chip. It was driving her crazy.

Her parents were at the kitchen table, papers spread in front of them. *Paul is home from work already?* she thought. This wasn't a good sign. Cassie's parents only asked to speak with her like this when something was really up. Like when she was little little and her hamster, Peteykins, had gotten really sick.

Uh-oh.

"Hey, Cass, how's it going?" Her dad stood up and gave her a kiss on the head.

"Great." Cassie bit her lip. "Um, guys, what's going on?"

"We wanted to talk to you about my job," her dad said.

Oh no! Paul must've lost his job. (Cassie called her parents by their first names, Sheila and Paul. She had total respect for them — they ruled! — but "Mommy" and "Daddy" was just so, well, *7th Heaven.*) Cassie was ready to tell him that everything would be okay, that she would limit her clothes buying, and that she would do everything she could possibly do to help, even if that meant not getting manicures and pedicures every other week.

"Your father got a promotion, Cassie."

"That is so amazing!" Relieved, Cassie sprang out of her chair and hugged her dad.

"But it means that he has to move — we all have to move," her mom added.

Cassie plunked into her chair, her stomach sinking. *Move? To a new neighborhood?* "Where?" she asked.

"To Maine, honey," her mother said gently. "All the way up north."

Cassie looked from one parent to the other in shock. How could this be happening? Just a few minutes ago, her biggest issue had been frizzy hair, and whether or not to run for class president. And now — *now* — Cassie couldn't even process it. Her stomach turned and her heart began to pound. Leave Houston and all her friends? She was about to cry, she could feel it.

"I know this must be really scary and disappointing, Cass," her father said. "But it's going to be okay, you know?"

"I know," Cassie said, her voice trembling, a big wave of tears working its way through her. "But Maine? Really?"

Her dad laughed. "I know. It's far. And cold. But Maine is beautiful. And there's a great school that wants you to start as soon as you can."

A new school? Cassie hadn't even thought of *that* yet.

Maybe it wouldn't be for a while. Maybe they were telling her now so she could really get ready over the next few months. "When?" she asked, her voice trembling.

"In two weeks. We wanted to wait until after the holidays to tell you."

Cassie couldn't help it anymore. Her big eyes filled with bigger tears. "Okay," she managed to say.

"Cass, we'll all be together. And you'll make friends there, too. You'll see." Paul smiled and walked to her.

"Your father's right, honey," Sheila said. "I promise."

Her parents both hugged her, but their reassuring words weren't helping Cassie feel any better.

"I'm going to go up to my room for a little while. Is that okay?" she asked, pulling away.

"Of course," Sheila said, petting Cassie's hair.

Before Cassie left the kitchen, she turned around. "I'm really proud of you, Dad." She hadn't called him that in forever, but she knew this was the right time.

Cassie closed her bedroom door and walked directly to her closet. She reached toward the back, behind all her shoes, and found him: Bobby the Teddy Bear. He'd been Cassie's teddy since she was two, and since Cassie was an only child, she secretly felt she could confide in Bobby as she would a sibling. Of course, *no one* knew that Bobby was still around.

Except for Erin.

Cassie slid off her marabous and sank onto her bed, holding Bobby tight. The tears came down and down and down. Moving to Maine! This was not supposed to happen. It just wasn't. Everything had been feeling so good. She was going to run for class president. She and her friends were going to *rock* the sixth grade. There was Donny McMahill's birthday party. Her mind raced. Maybe she could stay in Houston and live with Erin's family. That would be okay with the Donaldsons, she was sure of it. Maybe that would be the way to make this better. Cassie sat up, feeling a huge wave of relief.

But just as soon as she felt the relief, it went away. She couldn't be without her parents. She would miss them more than anything. Cassie plunked her head down on the bed, all cried out.

Her galloping thoughts were interrupted by the *ding* of her IM. Cassie gave Bobby one last hug and then sat down at her desk.

4EVERERIN: Okay, I'm over it. I swear.

Cassie smiled. What was she going to do without Erin?

MISSCASS: I'm so glad.

Cassie twirled her hair between her fingers. How was she going to tell Erin her awful news?

MISSCASS: I have something to tell you.

4EVERERIN: Celeb gossip???!
MISSCASS: No.
4EVERERIN: Newest gloss color?
MISSCASS: Uh-uh.
4EVERERIN: Okay. Last guess. New shoes?
MISSCASS: LOL! I wish!!!! Okay, are you ready?
4EVERERIN: You're scaring me. Is Bobby out?
MISSCASS: Yes.
4EVERERIN: Uh-oh. Okay. I'm ready.
MISSCASS: We're moving. Because of my dad's job.

Even writing it was hard. The tears filled Cassie's eyes again as she stared at the blank screen, waiting for Erin's response.

The phone rang.

Before Cassie could even say hello, Erin said, "Where?"

Cassie took a deep breath. "Maine."

Silence.

"Are you there?"

"I'm here," Erin said. "I can't believe it." Cassie could hear the tears in Erin's voice.

"Neither can I!" Cassie said, flopping back down on her bed.

Erin groaned on her side of the phone. "This *sucks*!" she said. "Isn't there a way you could get out of this? Oh, I know — you can move in with me and —"

"I can't do that, Erin. I thought about it, but . . ." Cassie sighed. "I mean, I know it's good for Paul and everything, but hello, did they even think of me at all?" Cassie knew the answer to that question. Of course her parents thought of her. But for the moment she just wanted to be whiny and complainy. "What am I even going to *do* in Maine?"

There was silence on the other end.

"Are you there?" Cassie asked.

"I'm here," Erin said, sounding determined. "I'm just Googling it. Let's see what I want to do when I come visit you."

A flicker of happiness went through Cassie. Leave it to Erin to look on the bright side of things.

"Ooh, we could rock climb!" Erin was trying hard.

"Can you rock climb in sparkly flats?"

"Hmm, good point. Hold on. I'm clicking on PERFORMING ARTS. . . . There's ballet! And theatre! Oh my God, they're doing a production of *Annie* right now! Cass! This is a good sign!"

They both laughed. Cassie and Erin could perform "It's the Hard-Knock Life" like no one else.

"Wow. People are going to *freak* when they find out," Erin said.

"I mean, some, I guess. Yeah."

"Don't even, Cass. You've been the most popular girl since the first grade."

Cassie blushed. "No, that's not true," she protested, even though, well, it was true.

"Cassie! Everyone adores you!"

Smiling, the tears welling up, Cassie just said, "Thanks." She thought for a moment. "Wait, *how* am I going to tell everyone? I *so* don't want to have to say it, like, a thousand times. There's not enough waterproof mascara in the world for that."

Both girls were quiet, thinking.

And then, Erin, brilliant genius that she was, said, "I know: Call Jen. Tell her. And tell her not to tell anyone. She has the biggest mouth in all of Texas!"

Cassie laughed. Jen really didn't know how to keep a secret. "Ooh, that's a good plan."

"You're going to be okay. And we're going to get you through this. I promise."

Cassie felt better. It wasn't going to be easy, but with friends like Erin, she knew she would survive. "I'm going to call Jen right now."

"I'll check in on you later," Erin said. Cassie was sure she was still looking for things for them to do in Maine when she came to visit.

"Thanks, you," Cassie said, the tears coming back.

“Please, thank YOU. Now no one will remember my little incident in the caf today!” Erin laughed. “Love you.”

“Love you, too.”

Cassie clicked the phone and dialed Jen’s number. And within a few hours, everyone knew. Cassie did her best to sound excited when her upset friends called her. But she was scared. Maine seemed so far away.

CHAPTER 2

Can You Wear Cute Shoes in a Snowstorm?

As Sheila drove up the long driveway to The Oak Grove School, Cassie's stomach flipped over. It was her first day at a new school in a new state, complete with a new weather pattern. The Knight family had moved just three days ago and *whoomp!* an enormous, welcome-to-Maine snowstorm had walloped them. Twenty-five inches of snow. Cassie didn't even know that was possible. Except for maybe in Antarctica or somewhere like that.

Sheila pulled up to the big, dark, castle-like building. Cassie had visited it over the weekend to pick up her class schedule and meet Principal Veronica, the way uptight leader of the school.

"Okay Cass, good luck, honey. I know this is going to be great. I do. Just give it some time."

Cassie had to admit that, despite being nervous, she was a little excited. She was going to meet so many new people. She looked out the window at the snow-covered lawn in front of her. There were kids everywhere, bundled up in puffy jackets, laughing and throwing snowballs at one another. *Snowball fights! Cool!*

"Thanks, Mom. It's going to be great!" Cassie smiled at her mother. This was hard for Sheila, too, she knew that. She gave her a big kiss and a hug. And with that, she opened the door and stuck one glamorous beaded flat out onto the ground.

Watch out, Oak Grove Middle School. Here comes Cassie Cyan Knight.

As she stepped out of the car, her foot slid out from underneath her and with a completely ungraceful *whoosh*, she landed — on her behind — in a snowbank.

Fabulous.

Sheila ran around the car to help her up. But Cassie was on her feet before her mother got there. "I'm fine. I'm fine." They looked at each other and laughed.

"Oh, Cass. Are you okay?" Sheila brushed snow from Cassie's new ugly down parka, which would have been embarrassing even without the big fall. "Honey, you have to let me buy you some good boots. You're going to break your neck. After school today, we're going straight to the mall."

The very thought of big clunky snow boots sent down Cassie's spine a chill colder than the subzero temperatures. But Sheila was right. She knew it.

"Okay," she said, distracted by the thought of what her hair looked like post–snow attack.

She hugged Sheila good-bye and walked into the school, careful not to have an additional spill. The hallway was so quiet, Cassie felt like she was in a cornfield in the middle of nowhere. No, wait: in a *library* in a cornfield in the middle of nowhere. It was all dark and musty and dusty. Oak Grove used to be a mansion that some family lived in.

Like, a haunted *mansion, maybe.*

When Cassie got to the principal's office, she smiled politely at the secretary behind the front desk. The whole place was all dark wood and dim light. There wasn't *one* splash of color or sparkle. As Cassie removed her parka, she felt like she practically glowed in the dark in her teal Chick by Nicky Hilton dress and flats.

The secretary was talking on the phone, obviously to a disgruntled parent. She didn't even look up at Cassie, just kept shaking her head and saying "mm-hmmm." Cassie gently cleared her throat. The woman looked up with a hideous, frightening glare and stuck her completely unmanicured pointer finger up in the universal "Just wait a minute, sister" sign. Cassie smiled as politely as possible.

Suddenly, Principal Veronica opened the heavy wood door. She wore a dark gray suit that she must have bought before Cassie was born. And worse, she had on unshined black shoes and her gray hair was in a messy bun. Another chill ran through Cassie.

"Hello, Principal Veronica!"

The principal looked Cassie up and down, seemingly stunned to see her.

"I'm Cassie Knight. Remember me?"

"How could I forget," she said, the corner of her mouth curling into a smile. She checked her watch. "You're late," she added sternly.

Cassie looked at the clock on the wall. She *so* wasn't late. But she wanted to make a good impression. And, besides, she didn't have the will to argue when all of her energy was being sapped trying to warm her feet up. "Sorry," she said, picking up her purse and following the principal out of the office.

Cassie walked alongside PV. That's what Cassie would call Principal Veronica from now on, at least in her mind. It just took the edge off her big, scary presence. And initials were *so* right now. She followed her through the narrow hallways. There was dark wood everywhere. The thin tan carpeting seemed to drink up sounds in the creepiest of ways. Unflattering yellow lights glowed from above, and Cassie was certain the glare turned her auburn locks carrot.

"At Oak Grove Middle School, we believe in educating the complete student, Ms. Knight. It is vital that education come not only from books and literature but also from the quest for self-knowledge."

Cassie did her best to stay focused. *Education was important. Yes, of course. Quest for self-knowledge? Wow, sure. But you know what else is important? A deep power-pack hair conditioner.* Cassie studied PV's unfortunate bun and rolled her eyes.

"Your homeroom is just up on the left," PV said.

I need to check my lip gloss and spray my hair before I meet people, Cassie thought. Before the move from Texas, she'd had one last cut and blowout from Fabrizio, her über-cool, über-rocking hairstylist. There were a lot of things Cassie was going to miss about Texas. But leaving Fabrizio had broken her heart.

"Is there a bathroom I can use before I go in?"

Principal Veronica looked at her watch for the third time since they'd been together. "Yes. Just to your left." She stopped walking, pointed to a varnished wooden door, and checked her watch. Again.

"Thank you so much. I'll just be a sec!" Cassie pushed through the door. The bathroom fixtures were old and cracked. Her shoes echoed loudly as she walked to the mirrors. The windows were open slightly, and outside, snowy hills rolled out far, far, far away. Cassie was so not in Houston anymore.

She reached into her purse for her cell, desperate to talk to one of her girls. But she stopped herself: new leaf, new life, *just relax*. Instead, she grabbed her most valuable tool from her purse: Cargo lip gloss. *LuLu Island, thank you very much.* She slid her finger over the dark side of the gloss, painted it onto her lips in two evenly pressured swipes, and then dipped into the light side. She smacked her lips together twice, a *thwack* echoing from the pale green tiles. She swiped her lashes with her Benefit BADgal Lash Mascara. *Roar!* Her lashes were fierce. Finally, she pulled out her hair spray and covered her red curls, scrunching them to new heights in a haze of super-holding goodness.

She smiled at the mirror, feeling much more like her old self. *It's time for a new adventure, Cassie.*

Refreshed, she did an about-face and marched

out of the bathroom. PV was waiting for her, tapping her poorly shod foot.

"Sorry about that!" Cassie smiled.

Taking a deep breath, she followed the principal into her new homeroom. It was much smaller than her classrooms in Houston. And there were no bright paintings on the plain white walls. It seemed so bare and dull.

Principal Veronica was talking to the teacher, who was in khakis and a white button-down shirt, buttoned too far up. Thick black curls framed his face and he had a big, toothy grin. He seemed young for a teacher, but nice. "Ms. Knight, this is Mr. Blackwell, your homeroom and English teacher," PV said crisply.

Cassie extended her hand. This was a major Life Rule for Cassie.

Life Rule #31: Shaking hands is a really mature, I'm-gonna-be-a-woman-who-runs-a-BIG-pretty-company thing to do!

He met her hand and shook it firmly.

"It's Robert. Robert Blackwell."

Cassie flushed with embarrassment. Oh no! All of this was so different and so new — a teacher offering his first name? It was one thing to call her parents by theirs. But a *teacher*? That was just crazy.

"You can call me Mr. B," Mr. Blackwell added.

"Hi, nice to meet you. You can call me Cassie."

Duh!

Embarrassed, Cassie ducked her head. She didn't know what to do with herself, her arms, her anything! She decided to rest her hand on her hip.

"I'll leave you here, Ms. Knight. I wish you luck in your academic pursuits." PV nodded briskly, then strode out.

Mr. Blackwell leaned against his desk and crossed his arms. He slid his smarty-pants oval glasses onto his head. "So, Cassie, welcome to Oak Grove. Tell us a little bit about yourself."

For the first time, Cassie turned her head and looked at her new classmates. She was frozen. Totally and utterly frozen. Thirty eyes were blinking at her through the pea-soup heat seeping from the radiators. She could feel her stomach doing cartwheels. She had to pull it together. Her eyes ran the length of the mahogany bookcase.

"Wow. You guys have a lot of books here!"

Jaws dropped.

"No! That's a good thing! Like, I mean, we had books, too, at my old school."

Uh-oh. This was not so perfect. Cassie had to find her way through this. She cleared her throat. "What I meant is that, in Houston, we had a lot of books and smart stuff, too."

Nothing. Not even eye contact from most people.

"I guess we just had more, like, sports trophies and things."

More jaws dropped. Cassie was sure her new classmates could see her heart beating through her satin dress. She took the moment of stifling silence to check out what the other students were wearing: gray. Gray, gray, and a little navy-blue. Sometimes, there was a "daring" splash of white or black. But the standard look for girls was: white turtleneck or button-down, navy blazer, gray skirt. And for boys, gray pants, navy sweaters.

Cassie felt a huge wave of homesickness.

Mr. Blackwell stepped in to save the day and became Cassie's favorite person in the universe when he said, "Cassie, why don't you have a seat at that desk over there?" He pointed to an empty desk near the back of the room.

Cassie began her walk, smiling as she did. All eyes were glued to her. She did her best to make eye contact and whisper hellos, but still only stony silence greeted her.

Finally in her seat, she dropped her bag on the floor and exhaled. She was exhausted, and the morning had just begun.

"All right, guys," Mr. Blackwell said, still leaning on his desk. "I want to make sure you all take care of Cassie. It's no fun being the new kid." He smiled out at the class. Cassie felt a prickle of relief. There *were* nice people in Maine.

Cassie fumbled through her bag to pull out a pen. She grabbed her favorite — teal, complete with silver glitter and a maribou tip. She smiled when she saw it, but then realized that no one at Oak Grove would appreciate it. She stuffed it back into her purse.

"Does anyone have any questions before we start our day?" Mr. Blackwell asked.

A girl raised her hand. She had pale skin, was wearing a gray fuzzy sweatshirt thing, and her brown hair was pulled tight into a ponytail. "I have a question," she said.

"Go ahead, Mary Ellen," Mr. Blackwell said.

"It's actually for Cassie. . . ." The girl turned in her seat to look at Cassie. "I'm Mary Ellen McGinty," she said sharply. Soon to be known as, Cassie would learn, *Mean, Mean Mary Ellen McGinty*.

"Hi," Cassie said, slightly relieved that someone was introducing herself.

"I know you're new here," Mary Ellen said, her lips forming a perfect heart. But when she next spoke, the heart broke. Into ten million pieces. "I'm just wondering why you aren't following dress code. It's an Oak Grove rule. We're not here for a fashion show, you know."

Now, THAT was apparent. And a real problem. Muddy snow boots were SO not on the runways this season, as far as Cassie could recall.

"I am in code!" Cassie gasped. "I'm wearing a dress that is at fingertip length," she said, jumping up and turning to the side, stretching her arm down so she could show that her hem was longer than her fingers. "I am not wearing any 'overly colorful' makeup." She put her hand to her cheeks to draw attention to her flawless application. "And I am wearing flats, which is far less than the two-inch maximum on heels."

"But we don't wear dresses. We just *don't*," Mary Ellen said, her words sharp.

Cassie gulped. They could take the sun away from her. Her friends. Her princess house. But her clothes? Never.

Oh no. Things were not going as well as she had hoped. Not at all.

CHAPTER 3

Hello, No Frozen Yogurt? Really?

Cassie was starving. She made her way into the cafeteria, surrounded by a sea of people she didn't know. And she was quickly learning that most of them didn't want to know her.

Her eyes quickly surveyed the caf. Long, wooden tables with worn-in plastic chairs, a gray marble floor, and brown trays. Like everything else about Oak Grove, it was colorless and blah. *I miss my Houston*, Cassie thought. She just wished she could sit with Erin and all the girls at their fave table, eating frozen yogurt and giggling.

Frozen yogurt! Cassie was newly inspired. That would bring her spirits up. She hoped they had the classic chocolate/vanilla swirl.

As she neared the counter, her eyes scanned for the frozen-yogurt machine. Soda machine: check.

Fridge filled with Snapple and Vitamin Water and water water: check. Little, cute, tiny fridge filled with little, cute, tiny ice creams: check. But Cassie was getting nervous. Where was the yogurt? Her eyes shot back and forth. Nothing! No FroYo! No oodles of sprinkles and crushed, delicious candy bars and cherries and other forms of deliciousness to top it all off!

It was official: This *was* a bad day.

Always a trooper, Cassie tucked her red tresses behind her ears, squared her shoulders, and took a deep breath; she'd been through tougher things than no frozen yogurt in her life. She headed to the sandwiches and picked up a turkey and cheese. It looked surprisingly edible. She made a mental check in her brain in the *Pros* column.

She grabbed a Coke Zero, smiled again at the thought of Erin and the girls back in Houston, and walked to the register to pay. She put her tray down on the ledge, balancing it with her hip. Just as she was opening her purse, the tray wobbled. Cassie panicked: Save the food or save the purse? Against her better fashion judgment, she opted for the food and both hands flew to the tray. And of course, her purse — and all of its contents, including lots of change — slipped out of her hands.

It all seemed to happen in slow motion. The purse flipped in the air, and her products, her mirror, her Arctic Chill gum, and her sunglasses flew everywhere. Cassie looked to the left and then to the right, and saw everyone in the cafeteria stop and stare. No. Not this. Not today! Cassie felt her face heat up, redder than her hair.

I've become Erin!

Maybe this was a mistake. Maybe she should have asked to be homeschooled. That would have been so much easier.

The woman behind the register, a kind, grandma type with curly silver hair, scurried around the counter to help Cassie collect her things. As she deposited a fistful of mascara, lip gloss, and cell phone into Cassie's purse, she looked at Cassie with big green eyes.

"First day?"

Cassie scrambled to pick up the glimmering change, some of which was still rolling away in various directions. She stood up, inexplicably out of breath.

"How'd you guess?"

The woman smiled. "Oh, I don't know."

"My unbelievable grace?" Cassie laughed at herself.

"Maybe that. Maybe the fact that no one here wears such beautiful colors as you do. I love your dress!"

"You do?" Cassie felt happiness wriggle through her. The lunchroom lady and Mr. Blackwell. That made two nice people in Maine. "Thanks so much! It's a Nicky Hilton!" A line was forming behind her. "Sorry, I should get out of your way," Cassie said, her eyes scanning the ground for any last evidence of her mishap. "How much is it?"

"It's on me," the woman said with a wink.

"Are you sure? Thank you so much!" Cassie grinned. "My name is Cassie Knight." She extended her hand.

"So nice to meet you. I'm Rose Miller."

"Oh! What kind of moisturizer do you use? Your hands are so soft!"

"Whatever's on sale at the grocery store," Rose said, smiling.

Cassie dug through her purse quickly, knowing she was making the line of people wait even longer for her. Finally, she found the small tube of L'Occitane Shea Butter Hand Cream, a product she thanked the goddess for each and every day, and gave it to Rose.

"You must try this. It will change your life!"

Rose took the tube and smiled. "You don't have to do that."

"Oh yes, I must! The fate of beautiful skin like yours can't be left up to supermarket sales! We must work to maintain it!" Cassie smiled again, picked up her tray, and walked out to the seating area, feeling ten times better.

But now, another problem: Where was she going to sit? This had *never* been an issue for Cassie, and it felt so weird to be in this new, awkward position. She looked out into a Milky Way of unfamiliar faces and bit her lip, her heart pounding.

She was certain no one was going to ask her to sit with them, so she would just approach a table.

Life Rule #37: When in doubt, be bold.

She surveyed her prospects, stopping for a moment at the napkin stand, praying to look less conspicuous. As she slowly pulled a napkin from the dispenser, she found her table of choice. Located at three o'clock sharp. Two girls were laughing together and seemed friendly. Like everyone else at Oak Grove, they wore navy blue sweaters over plaid and gray skirts. Who were they? Would they be her new Maine friends? She hoped so!

With new confidence, Cassie walked the length of the cafeteria, her target in focus at all times. When she neared the table, she widened her smile.

"Hi! I'm Cassie. Do you mind if I sit here?"

The laughter immediately stopped and the girls looked up in disgust.

"Yes."

This was a joke, right? It had to be. Cassie stepped closer to the table and put her tray down.

"So, what are your names?" she asked, her right fist scrunching up some curls.

"Our names are 'Go' and 'Away,'" one of them said.

"Tex-*as* girl," the other added with a twang.

Both girls laughed, their faces twisting into a very special form of hideousness.

Really? People actually acted like this in real life?

Cassie took a deep breath, the pressure of tears filling her eyes. *Do not let them see you cry.* She turned abruptly and began walking over to the first table she saw. She recognized some people from her homeroom, but she sat at the very end.

Cassie unwrapped her sandwich, taking far longer than she needed to get the plastic off. She didn't know what else to do. No one was really talking at the table and she wasn't sure why.

"So, do any of you guys have Mr. Blackwell for English?" she finally asked, careful of her accent. She hoped she didn't sound as twangy as that girl who'd made fun of her.

Of the six people at the table, only one looked up to acknowledge Cassie — a dirty-blonde with a tartan headband. "Everyone in sixth grade has him for English." She scowled at Cassie.

Is this for real? Or am I on one of those reality shows about mean kids? Cassie wondered.

"Well, I've only been at this school for, um, like, three hours," Cassie replied, hoping for some laughter.

But nothing. No one made a sound. They just ignored her.

Then, a prepped-out boy in an unseasonable pink polo turned to her and said, "You're from *Houston*?"

"Yes," Cassie responded cautiously.

"I've never met anyone from Texas," the boy replied.

"Looks like your luck has run out," another girl at the table muttered.

Cassie took a breath. "It's a nice state. The people are actually *friendly*." Cassie grabbed her purse, scooped up her tray, and said, "Thanks for letting me sit with you." As she turned to walk away, she felt the tears starting. There was no holding them back now. She caught her breath, placed her tray on the counter, and hurried to the *toilettes* again. (Cassie preferred the French word for *bathroom*.)

After carefully navigating the dark and long hallways, she ran into the Ladies and shut herself in a stall.

And burst into tears.

Her cell phone buzzed. She dug through her purse. It was a text from Erin.

Hope UR smiling!

Just the opposite, Cassie thought. Her heart melted as she realized what a good friend Erin was. Who needed new Maine friends?

Am now.

Cassie grabbed a tissue from her purse and carefully blotted her cheeks.

TNN. TNN. Tears Not Necessary.

After a makeup redux, Cassie headed to her locker. The lockers weren't even metal — they were that same old dark wood that was everywhere. (But they did allow more room for shoes. You never know when you might need a heel change in the middle of the day.) Cassie walked the quiet hallway, hoping she remembered her combination. As she ran the numbers through her head, she spotted a girl at a locker near hers. Cassie couldn't decide if she should say hello. Maybe she should just keep going.

But no, a Texas girl would never do that!

"Hi," Cassie said, trying to control her accent, so she didn't say *haaah.*

The girl — a super-pretty brunette in a surprisingly cool outfit — white blazer, cute gray skirt, and tortoise-shell glasses — jumped a little and clumsily slammed her locker shut. And just as she did, Cassie caught the glimmer of something sparkly in her locker.

Before she could say another word, the girl scurried away down the hall. Cassie sighed, her eyes on the locker. There was something good in there, and Cassie was going to find out what it was!

CHAPTER 4

Not Even the Mall Is Safe!

By the end of the day, Cassie was a fading flower. No one had spoken a word to her, except to comment on her Texas twang, which she didn't even know she had. The homework didn't seem like it was going to be more or harder than it was in Texas, just different. There *was* one thing Cassie decided she could manage in Maine: the schoolwork. Cassie had been an A student in Houston, and that was not going to change in Maine — regardless of how socially B-list she felt.

Cassie sighed as the bus carried her home through the snowy streets. She was so relieved to have the day behind her.

The bus let her off just in front of her house. She smiled at everyone as she walked past them and even said "Bye" to a boy and a girl she recognized from math class. They sort of smiled back, but didn't say anything.

What did I expect?

Before she hopped down the steps, Cassie turned her head and looked out at everyone, the dark green leather seats framing their heads. Then she glanced at the bus driver.

"Thanks so much." she said to him.

This was a major Life Rule.

Life Rule #46: You thank people for the work they do. Always.

"See you in the A.M.!" she added.

Even though Sheila had offered to drive Cassie to and from school, Cassie knew she had to take the bus no matter how nervous it made her.

Surprised, the driver smiled. "You, too!" he said.

Cassie walked down the steps, careful not to slip on the ice. She stopped for a moment to take in her new house. It was nothing like the old one. This house was an old farmhouse, built, in like, 1800 or something, drafty and old, stained gray with black shutters. There were blueberry bushes in the front yard, now covered with snow, but Paul said they would be really pretty in the summer. He said they could even eat the berries right from the bush. Cassie wasn't sure how she felt about that. What if there were bugs on them? *Gross.*

On the way up the front stairs, Cassie fumbled with her keys in her purse. *It's hard to use your hands when they're wrapped up in gloves.* Cassie hardly ever had to wear gloves in Texas.

Inside, the heat immediately soothing her, she put her bags down, took off her hideous parka, scrunched at her hair in the mirror, and ran up to her room. Well, it wasn't totally her room yet. All her stuff was there, but she hadn't Cassie-fied it yet. *Design Rule #51: A room must reflect its owner's sparkle.*

Before Cassie could settle in, her mom stuck her head into the room to see how the first day went and to announce that it was time to hit the mall.

"I have a vision for boots," Cassie said to Sheila as they walked through the mall, a place she finally felt at home. Cassie wanted something suede-y, nice and cozy on the inside, but nothing too Ugg-ish. Ugh to Uggs! Even girls in Texas wore them! Now, *that* was crazy.

Upon entering the shoe department, Cassie's eyes widened. Oh, *shoes.* They always had a dangerous effect on her! Her eyes flitted back and forth across all the styles and colors. So much to look at and choose from!

But Sheila was on to Cassie fast. "Earth to Cassie. We are here for *boots.* One pair of boots. And a pair of boots that you can actually wear in this ridiculous cold!"

Cassie looked up at her mom. She knew this was a hard move for Sheila, too.

"It is *so* cold! I had icicles on my face before when I was waiting for the bus!"

Sheila smiled. "Icicles, huh?"

"Totally!"

"C'mon, you." Sheila grabbed Cassie's hand and led her to the boots.

Even though Cassie and her mom had very different styles, they understood — and respected — those styles completely. Sheila was all *matchy-matchy* with sweater sets and pearls and stuff. Cassie was more *pizazz-y.*

Life Rule #2: You don't have to agree. But you do have to respect.

As she followed her mother, she caught sight of one of the most beautiful pair of boots that was ever created. Ever. Leather, with a lace-up back and gorgeously embroidered flowers up the side.

They were divine. Fast and furious, Cassie headed toward them, her hand outstretched, in serious need of a *TE* (textural experience). Just as she made contact and shivered in delight, something else caught Cassie's eye: Mary Ellen McGinty.

What was she supposed to do now? Cassie hated having weirdness with anyone, and this was going to be weird. She just knew it.

But she squared her shoulders, picked up the boot, and walked over to Mary Ellen, who was looking at the frumpiest pair of Keds Cassie had ever had the misfortune of encountering.

"Hi!" Cassie said.

Mary Ellen looked up with a grimace. "Oh, hi."

Cassie stuck the boot in between them, trying to make friendly conversation. "Have you seen these boots? Aren't they to die for?"

"Maybe if you're from Texas," Mary Ellen said coolly. "You're Cindy, right?" she snarled.

"No, I'm Cassie." *I mean, really?* Cassie knew Mary Ellen had said the wrong name on purpose. They had met just hours ago! "These boots are fabulous, no matter where you're from."

Mary Ellen rolled her eyes. "Cindy, you don't get it, do you? You're not the princess of Texas anymore. If you hadn't noticed, there are no runways around here. There's snow and ice — and pavement. So do yourself a favor and get a fleece and some real boots."

Cassie jerked back, worried that her hair might ignite from Mary Ellen's fiery words. No one had ever treated her this way. She wanted to ask Mary Ellen what a fleece was, but she was too startled to speak.

Finally, Cassie managed an icy "Have a good night." And with that, she flipped her hair dramatically and walked off to find a salesperson. She would try on the boots, no matter what Mean Mary Ellen McGinty had to say.

CHAPTER 5

So, Fine, This Isn't Going to Be a Fairy Tale

On Cassie's fourth day at Oak Grove, she gave in and decided to wear jeans. It was just too cold in Maine, and she needed to be smarter about her fabric choices. She chose a beautiful green peasant blouse with three teal flowers on the bodice and a pair of Sevens. Sevens, Cassie knew, are perfect when a girl needs some cheering up. Cassie wasn't *completely* depressed, but she needed some help. And her Sevens were always there for her. Not to mention the peasant shirt, which Erin had given Cassie last year for her birthday.

As Cassie entered Oak Grove, shivering and stomping snow off her lovely new boots, she wondered what Erin was doing right now, back in sweet ol' Texas.

There were exactly seven minutes to the first

bell and only one way to find out. Cassie ducked into the girls' room and shut herself in a stall. She pulled her cell phone out of her purse and smiled at the picture of herself with Erin on the main screen. Then she hit #1. Of course, Erin was the first person on her speed dial.

The phone rang almost one full time before Erin picked up. She must've been doing her hair or something.

"CCK? What's up?"

Cassie suddenly didn't know why she was locked in the stall again. It was so *dramatique*! She decided to go with it.

"I'm in a stall in the bathroom," she whispered, trying not to laugh at herself.

"Are you doing the drama thing right now?" Erin asked.

Cassie laughed. "Yeah, totally."

"Is everyone still being ridiculous and not noticing how utterly cool you are?"

"Kind of." Cassie sighed. It had been a lonely four days. "I just don't blend in." Cassie looked down at her vibrant shirt, suddenly convinced that it was fluorescent.

"So what?" Erin asked. "You are *not* a blender. You're Cassie. You ruled the school here in Houston. Remember?"

"I know. But *everything* is different here in Maine."

"But, Cass," Erin argued. "Don't change yourself to try and fit in, okay? I promise you everyone will see the light that is Cassie one day soon."

"All right," Cassie said, not quite convinced.

"Now, I have to go. I have rollers in my hair still and the bus is, like, going to be here in, oh no, ten minutes!"

"Rollers?!" Cassie squealed.

"I'm trying something new, okay? The girl with the prettiest curls is gone; it's free rein now."

"Oooh, really? Send me a pic later! You're going to look so good!"

"I will. Thanks!"

"Okay. Miss you!" Cassie said, loud enough that her voice echoed.

"Bye!"

Cassie stepped out of the stall, relieved that no one had come in during her pep talk with Erin. She stood in front of the mirror and applied just a little more Forest Green Lorac Eye Candy to her lids and a swoop of Pout Lip Polish on her lips. She pulled out her hair spray and covered herself in a fog of holding fumes. Just then a few older girls walked in, and as they passed Cassie, they waved their hands in front of their faces, batting the spray out of the way. Cassie rolled her eyes, made an about-face, and left. It was clear they had no idea what the purpose of hair spray was.

That afternoon, walking to the cafeteria for lunch, Cassie slowed down when she saw the Girl With the Sparkly Thing in Her Locker. Cassie had seen her a few times since that first day, but hadn't spoken to her.

Today, she decided to change that. There was something different about this girl. She didn't look or dress very differently from the others. But somehow she had . . . style.

When she got close, she said, "Hi. I'm Cassie." She extended her hand.

Looking surprised, the girl glanced up, her chestnut hair falling in a perfectly conditioned sheet across her face. *Finally*, Cassie thought. *Someone who conditions!* She had glasses on — sort of vintagey, sort of nerdy, somehow chic. "Hello. My name is Etoile."

Wow! Cassie had never heard a name like that.

"Can I ask you a question?" Cassie said hesitantly.

"Um, sure," Etoile said, smiling shyly.

"Well, the other day you had a tweed blazer-ey

thing on," Cassie began carefully. "It had really pointy lapels."

Etoile's face drained of all color. "What about it?" she whispered. She looked past Cassie, down the empty hallway.

"I was just wondering where you got it," Cassie said, certain she was on to something.

"Why?" Etoile crossed her arms over her chest, clearly suspicious.

"Because I loved it. It was so adorable."

"Really?" Etoile's face flushed. "Do you mean it?"

"Yes! Of course!"

"Well . . . I made it!" Etoile said, beaming.

"NO!" Cassie was awestruck.

Etoile nodded proudly. "I bought it in a vintage store and I totally redesigned it."

"That is so cool, Etoile." Cassie grinned, careful to say her name the right way.

"Do you think so? I was worried it might be too . . . *flashy* for Oak Grove."

"I bet," Cassie moaned. "There's no *color* at this school."

"Well, there wasn't — until you got here."

Cassie blushed. "But people look at me like I'm crazy."

"I know. But — oh, wait!" Etoile exclaimed. "Can I get your opinion on something?"

"Of course," Cassie said.

Etoile turned and fiddled with her locker. At first glance the inside was normal and blah, but then Cassie saw some of that mysterious sparkle. Etoile reached for it and held it out in front of her. It was a big swath of fabric — pink with white and blue crystals. It was totally amazing!

"Wow!" Cassie said.

"It's nice, right?"

"More than nice. Gorgeous. What's it for?"

"I was thinking about making a jacket out of it for spring. But I don't know."

"You have to — it will be incredible!"

"I just don't know if I can do it. I never really make my own stuff from scratch. I just fix things that I buy."

"I'll even help you if you need me to."

Etoile examined the fabric for a moment. "Really? Okay. I'm going to do it," Etoile said, carefully folding the fabric up into a square and putting it back in her locker. "Were you on your way to the cafeteria?"

"I was."

"Want to sit with me?" Etoile asked, pulling her backpack on.

"I'd love to." Suddenly, Cassie felt happier than she had since setting foot in Maine.

* * *

Cassie was so relieved to have purpose in the caf. After that first day, she'd been eating quickly by herself, pretending to catch up on homework. Today, Etoile chose a table by the window, which made Cassie happy. There was a little sun out and she was so glad to be able to enjoy it.

"Your name is really Etoile?" Cassie asked.

"Yeah. It means 'star' in French."

Cool, Cassie thought, unwrapping her sandwich. She was obsessed with France — she couldn't wait to be able to go someday.

"And I'm not telling you that because I want you to think I'm a star — or that my parents think of me that way or anything. Like, could they be more annoying than to name me that?" Etoile laughed at herself and covered her mouth. "And besides, when my parents see the grade on my latest math quiz, they *really* won't think I'm a star!" She laughed again.

"Are your parents French?" Cassie asked eagerly.

"No. Just slightly pretentious! We're from Maine."

"Well, it's still an awesome name."

"Thanks. But people always say 'E-toy-el' when they see it written out instead of 'Ay-twal.' It drives me crazy!"

"Well, I don't think I would ever be able to spell it, so at least I know how to say it!" Cassie smiled. "Really, it's amazing."

"You know what's *really* amazing?" Etoile asked.

"No — do tell!" Cassie sat up straighter in her chair.

Etoile dug through her backpack and pulled out a glossy magazine. She flipped through several pages and pointed to a pair of rose-colored, flowery flats. *Oh, divinity!* Cassie thought. Shoes like that would make any girl feel like Cinderella at the ball. "Are these killer, or what?" Etoile asked.

"I need those in my life," Cassie said, mesmerized.

Etoile put the magazine between them and moved her chair closer to Cassie's. She flipped another page and pointed to a celebrity dog dressed up for an event. "So cute! Look at that little tuxedo!"

Cassie giggled at the silly dog. It felt good to laugh in school again.

As if reading her mind, Etoile looked up at her. "How have your first few days at Oak Grove been?"

Cassie sighed. "It's so different than what I'm used to."

Etoile looked at her in complete understanding. "You'll get the hang of it. It must be really different from Texas."

"It *really* is!" Cassie took a bite of her sandwich, and Etoile flipped the page again. "So, can I ask you a question?"

"Okay."

"Well, I can't point right now, but can you tell me who two people are?"

"Sure."

Cassie looked back over her shoulder at the two girls who wouldn't let her sit with them on her first day. Mary Ellen was sitting at their table today. Cassie had done her very best to avoid any contact with Mary Ellen since the mall incident. She slowly turned back to Etoile, hoping she was being nonchalant.

"Those girls sitting with Mary Ellen," Cassie whispered. She took another bite of her sandwich.

"You mean the Nightmare Sisters? Lynn Bauman and Deirdre Donahue. Don't think twice about them. They are totally the founders of the Mary Ellen Fan Club. They are so obnoxious!"

Cassie laughed. "The Nightmare Sisters? That's genius!"

And as she and Etoile laughed together, Cassie knew that she had found her first friend at Oak Grove.

CHAPTER 6

Can You Say "Friday?"

That Friday, Cassie was completely relieved. At last, this first, unbearable week would be behind her. It *had* to get easier after this.

She hurried to the gym for a special assembly and stopped short when she walked in. The gym was filling up. There were kids everywhere, clamoring for spaces in the bleachers, and Cassie felt beyond intimidated. Her phone buzzed in her purse — a LeSportsac, designed by this rad graphic artist, with all of these sweet blue birds all over it.

Cassie discreetly pulled out her phone and looked at the screen. It was a text from Etoile!

Sit with me! ★

Signed with a star! It was so adorable.

Cassie looked up at the bleachers and finally, like a lighthouse on the edge of the stormiest of beaches, she saw Etoile.

Maybe her week hadn't been *so* unbearable.

Cassie wove her way up the bleachers, stepping around people and over backpacks, her boots thumping against the wooden planks.

"What's up?" Cassie said when she reached Etoile.

"Hey!" Etoile said, smiling and patting the space next to her.

"So, what's this assembly about?" Cassie asked, arranging herself and her stuff on the seat.

Etoile rolled her brown eyes. "They do this all the time. You never know what it's about." She pulled out a bag of dried fruit. "Here," she said, pushing the bag toward Cassie.

"Thanks." Cassie put her hand in and extracted a banana chip and a piece of mango. No one at school in Houston ever had dried fruit in their bag. Cassie took a bite. *Delicious*!

Life Rule #98: Always try new things—you never know, you might like them!

Just then, the microphone squealed, setting Cassie's hair on end. Principal Veronica stood under the basketball net, the amp in front of her. She was dressed in a blue grandma suit and black flats, with an unmatching blue band in her hair. *Oh, poor thing!* thought Cassie.

"Good morning, Oak Grove ladies and gentlemen. It's a brand-new semester, and I hope you all are settling into your new routines beautifully. I just wanted to take a moment to say hello to all of you and wish you very well. It's been a wonderful school year thus far and I hope it only gets better and better. . . ."

Cassie was zoning out when she felt a tap on her leg. When she looked down, she saw a notepad on the bench between Etoile and her. There were two words written on it:

HELP US

Cassie caught a laugh before it escaped. She picked up the pen and slowly wrote:

I WISH I KNEW HOW

She looked up. PV was going on. ". . . because there is nothing like the joy of academics. You are only starting on your academic journey. And for some of you, your lives will be filled with schooling. Fine schooling. You know who you are. . . ."

Cassie looked down at the notebook. Etoile's next entry was simply:

☹

PV droned: "Harvard, Yale, Princeton! I am so excited for your futures, Grovians!"

Cassie picked up the pen:

Did she just say "Grovians"?

"Now," PV said, the mic echoing, "I would like to introduce Mr. Robert Blackwell, who has some wonderful things to share with you."

From the crowd, some of the boys shouted, "Mr. B!"

Mr. Blackwell walked to the mic, and Cassie smiled to see her energetic teacher. "Hey, guys. How's your Friday?"

A bunch of "whoops" and "good"s came from the bleachers.

"Good. Really good. You all sound really excited to be here."

Everyone laughed.

"So, I want to talk to you about this year's annual fundraiser. Now that Rebecca McGinty has graduated, we have a lot of work to do. I need you all to stay focused on it, okay?"

The room was silent.

"Guys? Hello? Do you hear me? Okay?"

Finally, the room responded with murmurs and nods.

Cassie looked at Etoile. "What is *it*?" she whispered.

Mr. Blackwell continued, "So, if you want to be on the committee, you should speak to Mary Ellen McGinty, our student rep, or me about it. Mary Ellen, do you want to come up and say a few words?"

Etoile rolled her eyes. "A Mary Ellen project," she whispered back.

Mary Ellen stood up from the front row and walked to the mic. She took a moment before she started to speak and cleared her throat. Then, in the cheeriest voice Cassie ever had the displeasure of hearing, she said, "Hi, I'm Mary Ellen McGinty. And I want to make sure you all take part in the charity fundraiser this year!"

Cassie was shocked. Stunned! Was this the Mary Ellen McGinty that she saw at the mall who couldn't even lower herself to share the beauty of a boot?

Cassie stared at Mary Ellen standing at the mic, her shoes brown and drab, her complexion tight from an overly astringent cleanser. Really, too bad. Because her skin was . . . No! No! Cassie would not feel bad for this girl. No! Stop!

"I will be arranging a meeting next week to get everything started. And please don't come to the meeting unless you really are committed to working hard. The charity fundraiser was my sister Rebecca's idea. And now that she's graduated, I need real team players who can help me realize it for the third year." Mary Ellen took a stupidly dramatic breath. And then, "In a row."

With that, she smiled out at the crowd and the Nightmare Sisters began to clap. The rest of the room quickly followed.

Mr. Blackwell stepped forward. "Before we end, I just want to make sure no one has any questions."

Cassie wanted to ask for more details. And she wouldn't have thought twice about it if Mary Ellen weren't up there, waiting to pop out her unmanicured claws. The Cassie of just a month ago wouldn't let that stop her, though. She rubbed her hands together quickly to warm them up, and scrunched her curls. She stood up. Etoile was staring at her in disbelief.

"What's up back there, Cassie?" Mr. Blackwell asked.

"Mr. B, I'm sorry, but I don't know what the fundraiser is," Cassie said.

"Oh, of course!" Mr. Blackwell said. "Mary Ellen? Would you please tell Cassie about it?"

Mary Ellen turned to face the crowd, her eyes dark now — stormy — as they surfed the bleachers for Cassie. "My sister started it three years ago because we wanted to do something to help the environment," Mary Ellen said crisply. "And so, each year, we plant fifty trees on campus and raise money for the National Arbor Day Foundation with a bake sale. It's always been *very* successful."

Cassie smiled and nodded. A bake sale? That all sounded so boring. Totally good and the right thing to do but *boring*.

"Does that help, Cassie?" Mr. Blackwell asked.

Cassie smoothed her shirt and said, "Actually, I have a question." She bit her lip, knowing she was about to anger Mary Ellen further. "I know I don't know much about Oak Grove but . . . why are we planting *trees* for charity?"

Mary Ellen shot a glare at Cassie, scowled, and stepped closer to the mic. "Maybe you don't know about the environment back in Texas, but our planet is in serious danger of succumbing to something called the greenhouse effect." Mary Ellen spoke deliberately slowly, like she was addressing a five-year-old.

Cassie gritted her teeth. She had not been the secretary of the Environmental Club in Houston by accident. "It's Mary Ellen, right?"

Mary Ellen was thrown off by the question.

Cassie repeated herself and said again, slowly, like they do on soap operas, "Your name is Mary Ellen, right?"

"Yes," Mary Ellen said, confused.

"Hi, I'm Cassie."

Confused no more and back to her nasty self, Mary Ellen said, "I know. We've already *met*."

"I know we did," Cassie replied. She caught her breath and made sure she was staying calm and considerate — but to the point. "I just wanted to be polite and reintroduce myself before we had what might be our first public disagreement." Cassie swallowed hard, staying as calm as she could, holding her hair for a moment in a twist and then letting the red curls fall gracefully down her back.

Etoile fidgeted in her seat, and so did everyone else. Hello, drama!

Before she began, Cassie pushed her turquoise bangle to the top of her arm, so it wouldn't jangle around. "I am well aware of the greenhouse effect,

Mary Ellen. Thanks for reminding me — for reminding all of us — because, well, you can never be reminded enough of such environmental travesties. I'm just wondering why we're planting trees in *Maine*." She paused and looked around at her new classmates. "While I think there are a lot of things missing here, there's one element that I am certain is plentiful: trees." Cassie looked around the gym — the cavernous, oh-no-what-am-I-doing-the-whole-school-is-looking-at-me gym.

There were whispers. Cassie felt slightly nauseated. At least her green face matched her turquoise flowered tunic. Sometimes her mouth got the better of her.

"Wow, that's a good point, Cassie. Do you have another idea?" Mr. Blackwell asked, stepping slightly in front of Mary Ellen.

Cassie twisted her hands together. "Um —"

Just then, Mary Ellen, hands in tight fists at her sides, snapped like cheap spaghetti. "Well, until you have a better idea, maybe you should keep your mouth shut." She stamped her foot, her blue eyes blazing.

Cassie didn't want this to be a fight. She didn't want to come across as a troublemaker. She just wanted to help make something better. She put her head down, thinking, her colors loud against all the muted tartans and beiges around her.

And then, just then, she had an idea. The best idea ever.

She lifted her head.

"What if we raised money to buy saplings for communities throughout the country — the world — that needed them more than we do?"

"What?" Mary Ellen hissed.

Cassie could feel the vibe in the gym change — she was suddenly surrounded by softly growling, drooly, Mary Ellen watchdogs. Badly accessorized watchdogs, baring their teeth at Cassie.

"Mary Ellen, please don't think I'm trying to change anything," she stammered. "I'm not. But sometimes, a new eye on something really changes how you think about it."

"Tell us more, Cassie," Mr. Blackwell said. "What does your new eye see?"

It all came to Cassie in a wave, like most of her good ideas — including the one that had led Sheila to get caramel highlights.

"What if we did a charity fashion show?" she burst out, her cheeks flushing. Her heart started to beat faster, not because she was nervous, but because this *was* a good idea. "We could ask people to buy tickets to see the show. We could even invite newspapers and stuff to come to our big event!"

The entire gym fell silent. Cassie looked down at Etoile. She was pale but smiling enormously. Too bad no one else was.

Before Cassie could slump back down in defeat, Mr. Blackwell stepped closer to the mic. "Cassie, that's a terrific idea. I'll talk it over with the faculty and we'll see if it's something we'd like to consider."

"Okay, thank you." Cassie nodded, sitting back down.

"That was genius," Etoile whispered to her, but Cassie could only sigh. Based on the cold looks her other classmates were giving her, she was sure no one else felt that way. Not even Mr. Blackwell. He was probably just being nice.

CHAPTER 7

Sh-8-kn in My Pumps

By Monday, Cassie assumed that everyone would have forgotten all about the assembly. But Mr. Blackwell asked her to stay behind after homeroom.

"How has everything been going?" he asked.

"It's good!" Cassie said, not really wanting to have another *How are you, New Kid?* conversation.

"Glad to hear it. I wanted to let you know that we discussed your fashion show idea in our faculty meeting on Friday."

The butterflies started waking up in Cassie's stomach. "Oh, really?" she said, trying to keep calm.

"And we all loved it. We think it's fresh and exciting and will really be a great event for Oak Grove. And we'd like to do it this year. Can you meet with us today after school to tell us more?"

Cassie was speechless. They'd *liked* her idea?

"But . . ." she began, her pulse racing. "What about . . . Mary Ellen? Does *she* like the idea?"

"I wouldn't worry too much about Mary Ellen. We never said we were definitely doing things the same way this year. We'll talk to her after everything is finalized and she'll come around. She has to — she's been on the committee forever."

"Okay," was all Cassie could say.

"Really, it's going to be fine. There are far more important things for you to think about. You're psyched, right?" Mr. B asked enthusiastically.

Cassie had to admit that she was. "I am really excited!"

"Great. So are we. So, do some thinking today before the meeting, if you can. Sound good?"

"Sounds great!" Cassie walked away from Mr. B, a huge smile on her face. This was going to be amazing!

But as the day went on, Cassie found herself tippie-toeing through the halls. Even when she was telling Etoile the news during lunch, she whispered, afraid that someone would overhear. And she made Etoile promise to keep it quiet!

After lunch, Cassie decided she needed some

major reinforcement. She pulled out her cell and texted Erin:

Sh-8-kn in my pumps

It didn't matter that Erin didn't know the latest development. She would still send Cassie nice, big, twenty-gallon Texas vibes. And Cassie needed as many as she could get! She felt like a total school-wrecker.

Cassie was so relieved she'd worn an especially perfect outfit, consisting of one of the most confidence-inducing items in her collection: a super-fab frock she scored from a vintage shop in Houston. And this dress was a beauty: coffee and cream paisley swishes, set against an inky purple. *Design Rule #17: Personal style should always be of the moment, with a wink at the future and a grateful nod to the past.*

Cassie knew her confidence would falter the moment she entered English class. Mary Ellen was going to be there and it was going to be awkward. What if Mr. B said something to her in front of everyone?

She ducked into the *toilettes* and gave a good spray of the hair just before class, then took a deep,

deep cleansing breath as she walked into the room.

Everything seemed normal. Mr. Blackwell was at his desk; the windows were open to let some cool air in over the steamy haze of the radiators; kids dressed in gray and beige sat at their desks.

Mary Ellen was talking with the Nightmare Sisters. As Cassie settled into her seat and got herself ready for class, she avoided eye contact with Mary Ellen at all costs.

"Good afternoon, guys," Mr. Blackwell said. "I thought we could start class with a quick and easy writing exercise. You can write about anything you want. Anything at all." He paused for a moment and smiled. "But there's just one catch. You only have five minutes." He looked down at his watch. "Okay, go."

Just as Cassie's pen hit her notebook, she heard someone speak. Well, not just someone. Mary Ellen.

"Excuse me, Mr. Blackwell?" she said.

Cassie popped her head up, along with every other person in the classroom, like gophers from their holes.

"Yes?"

"Before we begin writing, I just wanted to ask a business question."

Mr. Blackwell crossed his arms. "Shoot."

"I was wondering if you could tell the class what you and I discussed earlier today?"

Mr. Blackwell didn't miss a beat. "I don't think this is an appropriate time, Mary Ellen."

Cassie hoped this wasn't what she thought it was.

Mary Ellen looked hesitant, but then she plowed ahead. "But, Mr. Blackwell, I am the student rep and I want to know what the students think about the new idea for the annual fundraiser." Mary Ellen turned and glared at Cassie.

"Well," Mr. Blackwell started, seemingly unpetrified by Mary Ellen's wrath. "Like I told you, we are having a *faculty* discussion today." He looked out at the class. "As you all know, a new idea has been thrown into the ring for this year's fundraiser. And we would like to take the time to review that."

"The *fashion show* idea?" one of the Nightmare Sisters asked.

"Yes. Cassie's plan for a charity fashion show." Mr. Blackwell pulled his glasses up on his head.

Cassie didn't know what to do. All eyes in the

classroom were split between looking at her and looking at Mary Ellen.

"To be honest," Mary Ellen said, "I don't think most people would want to do a fashion show." Mary Ellen craned her neck around to see Cassie. "Right, guys?" Mary Ellen asked the room. "Don't you all agree?"

The room was silent. The radiator hissed. A tiny breeze blew in through the windows. In unison, the Nightmare Sisters said, "I agree."

And then, suddenly, the class was filled with robotic murmurs of agreement. Mary Ellen triumphantly nodded her head.

"People have different interests, you know," Mr. Blackwell said. "It's what makes the world go 'round."

"Really? I thought being smart and successful and giving back to the community was what made the world go *'round.* Not hair spray and tacky dresses."

The Nightmare Sisters snickered.

Cassie wrapped her arms around herself, protecting her dress from such rude words.

"Mary Ellen, let's watch our mouths, okay?" Mr. Blackwell said.

"Do *you* like fashion, Mr. Blackwell? Do you care

about a fashion show? Would any *boy* in this room care?" she snapped back.

Silence crawled through the room like an icky snake.

C'mon! Cassie wanted to cry. *She's playing the boy card! Boys are way too shy to admit that they like to get dressed up and stuff.* But Cassie decided to keep her mouth shut. A new Life Rule was forming. It was something like, *Sometimes it's better to not say anything at all.*

Just then, her phone buzzed in her Jordache bag. She reached for it, against all better judgment.

Life Rule #21: No techno-thingies in class. Just rude. And pointless. You're in school to, well, learn.

But this was an emergency. She slid the phone out. It was a text from Erin:

Ms. Cassie Cyan Knight never sh-8-ks!

Everything changed at that moment for Cassie. There was no point in being scared of Mary Ellen. Or of anyone. Fine, she had only been at Oak Grove for a week, but that didn't mean her idea wasn't a good one. She stood, her knees pushing her up just a second or two before her mind was ready.

Darn! That always happens!

"Excuse me," Cassie said, her voice more powerful than she expected it to be.

All heads turned.

"Since the faculty is going to decide today, I think we should just let them worry about all of this," she said. "And, just so you know, Mary Ellen, I have been asked to go to the faculty meeting to talk about my idea."

Mary Ellen's fists clenched. One of the Nightmare Sisters gasped. Cassie wasn't yet sure which was Lynn and which was Deirdre.

"And if you'd like to join us for the discussion, then I'd love to see you there."

More gasps in the room.

And with that, Cassie scrunched some curls, sat down, picked up her Deery Lou pen and began to write.

But she *was* worried. What if the faculty thought the fashion show was a terrible idea? What would she do then? No one at Oak Grove would ever take her seriously if that happened.

Cassie swallowed hard and did her best to concentrate on her work, but her worries continued to plague her.

CHAPTER 8

With So Much to Say, Why Is There No One to Talk to?

Cassie paced outside the school, waiting for Sheila to pick her up. She'd missed the bus so she could attend the faculty meeting, and now, she was bursting to talk to someone! Erin was in ballet class back in Houston and all the other girls were probably still at their extracurriculars. And Etoile wasn't picking up her phone! How could there be no one to talk to? *This is the twenty-first century, people!* she thought.

She looked up at the big Maine sky, the cold wind against her face, her feet freezing in her boots.

When she glanced back down, she saw her mom's car turn onto the long driveway. She watched the blue car get bigger and bigger as it came closer. She could see Sheila behind the wheel with her sunglasses on.

Cassie popped into the car. Before she could even slam the door, Sheila slid her sunglasses onto her head and asked, "So?"

Cassie wanted to play it coy. Even for a minute. "Yes?" she said.

"Are we throwing a fashion show?" her mother said, clapping her leather-gloved hands together in excitement.

"Can we go to the mall?" Cassie asked. "I really want to get more scarves and stuff. This cold weather is crazy!"

"Cassie Cyan Knight, you stop toying with my emotions."

Cassie squealed. "Yes!" she said. "Yes! We are throwing a fashion show!"

Sheila threw her arms around Cassie. "Oh, honey! This is wonderful. I am so proud of you!"

Cassie hugged her mother back hard. Nothing was better than a good hug. "I can't believe it!" she said, her mouth shmushed into her mother's hair.

"Tell me everything!" Sheila said as she put the car in drive.

"Well, I went into the meeting right at three, and all these teachers were sitting there. The room was chocolatey wood with leather chairs and stuff — it was so official. And Mr. Blackwell sat nex[illegible] me. And he introduced me and I talked about my id[illegible] and everything. And then PV was like, 'I think it is a marvelous idea!' *Marvelous!* I didn't even know people really, like, said that word. And so they want to do it!"

"Oh, honey, that's wonderful. It's . . ." Sheila looked at Cassie and together they both cried, "MARVELOUS!"

By the time they got to the mall, Cassie had told Sheila all the details of the meeting. And she never once mentioned Mary Ellen (who had been a total no-show). She didn't want to ruin her excitement by worrying about Miss Meanie.

They walked to the food court to get bottles of water before they started. They knew all too well that they had to stay hydrated while shopping! As they waited in line to pay, Cassie saw Etoile sitting at a table with her mother. It must have been her mother — she had that same chestnut-y hair.

Cassie handed her water to Sheila. "That's Etoile! I'll be right back!" She ran straight to them, her boots clunking against the marble floor.

"Etoile!" she shouted as she ran.

Etoile looked in Cassie's direction. When she saw her, she stood up, her face filled with anticipation.

“Ca[illegible] What happened?”

I tried calling you but couldn’t get through!” When she got to Etoile they hugged.

“What did they say?” Etoile’s eyes were big and bright.

“Well . . .” Cassie said teasingly.

“C’mon! I’m dying to know!”

Cassie smiled big. “They said yes! They said they thought it was the best idea they’d heard in a long time!”

“I knew it!” Etoile said. “You’re the best!”

Cassie’s eyes filled with the happiest tears and she hugged Etoile again. Arms tight around each other, the two girls bounced up and down, squealing.

Sheila walked over then. “Let me guess, you’re Etoile’s mom?”

The woman laughed. “I am. And you’re Cassie’s?”

“I am!”

The two girls unlocked from each another.

“Mom!” Etoile said. “This is Cassie and her mom!”

Cassie shook Etoile’s mother’s hand. “Mom!” Cassie said to Sheila. “This is Etoile’s mom and Etoile, my executive vice president of the entire show!”

“What? Really?”

"Of course!" The girls shrieked ag
hugged.

"I have an idea. Why don't you two go shopping and meet up back here in an hour?" Etoile's mother asked.

"Perfect." Etoile said. "I can teach Cassie what a fleece pullover is."

Cassie scrunched her nose. It just sounded so terrible.

"Cassie, you better come back with something warm and Maine-ready," Sheila said, handing her some money.

"And some nail polish?"

"ONE bottle only," Sheila laughed, and the two girls ran off together.

As they shopped, Cassie and Etoile worked out a plan for the show. Cassie was afraid she was going to have to convince Etoile to be on the committee, but she said yes right away. They decided they would have sign-ups at lunchtime tomorrow, and then have their first meeting. First they would assign each person to a committee like accessories, skirts, and set design. Then they would ask stores at the mall to donate clothes to the show. Etoile even offered to ask her friend Jonah, who was the best artist in the school, to do the set building.

ate their brilliant ideas, the two girls to get serious about some shopping. Soon sie was surrounded by a pile of clothes in a dressing room, directly across from Etoile's. As she navigated the pile of picks, Cassie had another idea, maybe the best one of the night. She just needed Etoile to agree to it.

"I have one more thing I'd love for you to do for the fashion show," Cassie called out to Etoile through the dressing room door. She was trying on a darling Guess? top.

"Okay, what is it?" Etoile asked, pulling on a pair of corduroys.

"I want you," Cassie said, poking her head through the top of the shirt, "to design that fantastic jacket for the show and premiere your talent to the world."

Etoile was silent. Then Cassie heard her friend say, "Are you crazy?"

Cassie fluffed her hair and opened the door, just as Etoile opened hers.

Even though she was flustered, Etoile couldn't help herself. "Caah-ute! You have to get that!"

Cassie did a little spin. "Are we sure?"

"Totally sure. What about these?" Etoile asked, going up on her toes.

"Like, perfection. Really. Get them!"

Etoile stepped back to the mirror an
herself out. "Okay."

"And, you *are* going to make that jacket for the show. You don't have a choice."

Etoile crossed her arms over her chest. "Cassie, I just can't. Thank you so much for thinking of me that way. But it's too much pressure." Her eyes were big and pleading.

Cassie shut the door to change. "Okay, how about this?" she said through the door. "You make the jacket and we decide then if it's going in the show? Okay?"

Etoile was silent.

"I'm going to count to three. And if you stay quiet, I will just have to assume that it's a yes." Cassie stood, not moving, hoping she wouldn't get a response. "One . . . two . . . three."

She fluffed her hair and opened the door. Etoile stood there, her arms full of clothes, grinning.

"Yay," Cassie said, her heart bursting. She leaped forward and gave Etoile a giant hug.

"Yay," Etoile said and hugged Cassie back.

CHAPTER 9

Rope Climbing Is So Not a Fashion Statement

The next day, Cassie was planning on being all business. She had to be. There was a lot of work to be done and not much time to do it! Whatever Mary Ellen had to say, Cassie knew she had a job to do. And that job was to create the most successful fundraiser ever! To mentally prepare, Cassie wore one her favorite outfits: a black and white checked Betsey Johnson dress with a black bolero and a pair of red pumps that were just heavenly.

Her mind was reeling as she sat in homeroom. So much was happening so quickly. She pulled her marabou pen out of her purse and began a to-do list while she waited for Mr. B.

Just as the glitter ink rolled onto the paper, Mr. B walked into the class with Mary Ellen. She looked really upset.

Oh no. She must have gotten the news about the show.

Cassie didn't want her to be mad about it, but there was nothing she could do. After a good shop last night, Cassie, Etoile, and their moms had a solid powwow over some FroYo (finally!) and all of them agreed: Let Mary Ellen be upset and give her some space.

"Good morning, everyone," Mr. B said as he unpacked his worn leather briefcase. "I want to let everyone know some news about the fundraiser. This year, we have decided to take the project in a new direction and hold a charity fashion show. And, as you can probably guess, Cassie Knight back there is going to head up the student committee." He gestured to Cassie. "So if you want to sign up, you should speak with her." He stopped and smiled at Cassie. "Is there anything you want to say, Cassie?"

Cassie sat up straight and folded her hands on her desk. She didn't know she was going to be asked to say something so soon, but that was okay, she was ready.

"I just want you all to know that I am so excited to do this. And if anyone wants to be a part of it, just let me know. There's room for everyone!" she said. She turned toward Mary Ellen, hoping she was smiling, ready to be a part of it all, and volunteer a design idea.

But of course not. The room was silent. Mary Ellen didn't even acknowledge her. Cassie continued on. "So, if you want to sign up, just stop by my table at lunch and we can take it from there. Our first meeting will be tomorrow after school."

"Principal Veronica will be making an all-school announcement today, so be on the lookout for that," Mr. B said. "And don't be thrown off by the fashion part; we need all hands on deck for this. This is a fundraiser. It's not only about the clothes."

"Well, it sort of *is* about the clothes," Cassie said truthfully. "But the other stuff is super-important, too," she added with a grin.

No one laughed.

Would she *ever* get through to her classmates? Ever?

Third period was gym class. Dreaded, hated, hideous, and horrible gym class. It's not that Cassie had any problem with sweating and running and being healthy and stuff. Of course not. *Duh, being healthy, like, makes you live longer.* (This was not yet a Life Rule, but she realized she needed to make it one soon. She just needed to work out the exact language.) And she loved her gym outfits. Today's featured two wristbands, left arm white, right arm blue, her Grid Propel Plus Sauconys with delicious blue laces, and her pearl Danskin unitard with her midnight Cobweb Crop Tie-Front Sweater and matching skirt. And matching leg warmers, of course.

But here were the bad things, and there were a lot:

1. Getting all sweaty.
2. Getting all sweaty with other people. Especially boys. They <u>really</u> get all sweaty.
3. The things you have to do! Like swinging a bat, or running in circles, or the worst: throwing a ball.
4. I mean, hair!!! What's a girl supposed to do with her hair when she has, like, ten minutes to de-sweat, re-glamor, and bejewel?
5. Feeling kind of clammy and sticky for the rest of the day. So not cute.

Cassie walked into the locker room and put her backpack in a locker. She pulled out her gym fashions and changed. There were girls around her, laughing and talking, but she couldn't think of a word to say. They were talking about such boring things, like debate club and what they thought was going to be on such-and-such quiz.

She sat on the bench to put on her leg warmers and slouch them just so. While she did, someone walked toward her and stopped. Cassie looked up and saw a pair of pasty white legs.

Oh, this was going to be Mary Ellen. It had to be.

And it was not going to be good.

Cassie sat back and looked up. The flourescent light glowed above Mary Ellen. The Nightmare Sisters stood behind her, looking more green in the bad lighting and gym gear.

A Texas girl always starts out polite. "Hi there!" Cassie put her hands on the bench and crossed her legs. She worked hard not to wrinkle her nose when she saw what Mary Ellen was wearing. A pair of hideous boys' soccer shorts and a big, dingy white T-shirt. *Aaaaaagh!* This fashion situation was worse than Cassie thought.

"Hi there," Mary Ellen said back, mockingly. Some girls stopped talking.

"What's going on?" Cassie asked, her heart picking up speed.

"I know fashion's your thing and all," Mary Ellen began.

Cassie stood, her sweater and skirt overly adorable. The other girls were blatantly staring now. "It's one of my things, yes," she said, putting her hand on her hip.

Mary Ellen went on. "You know, we really try to take gym seriously here. I thought you would have at least figured *that* out by now." She gave Cassie the old up-and-down eyes.

Cassie knew she was SO NOT the one who should be looked up and down in this situation!

"I try hard to excel in all areas, so I'm ready!" Cassie said. "What are we playing today?" Cassie was trying to sound tough, but she didn't want a gym showdown. She knew herself. Gym wasn't her strongest suit.

"We're climbing ropes today."

Climbing ropes? What's the point? Where are we going? To the ceiling?

The bell rang and the other girls ran into the gym. Mary Ellen gave Cassie one final look and walked away.

All of Cassie's hopes and dreams of a successful fashion show seemed to slip out of her hands. What had she been thinking? She would never get people on her side.

When she entered the gym, she saw four ropes hanging from the ceiling. Kids were lining up at each one, ready to take turns climbing up and down. Cassie had never seen such a thing before. They did square dancing and aerobics and fun stuff in her Houston gym class. Nothing that involved ropes!

When it was her turn, all eyes were on her. She knew Mary Ellen's were, for sure. For super sure.

Maybe she would perform better under pressure.

Or maybe not.

By the time she got halfway up the rope, which was surprisingly easier than she thought it would be, she became nervous. The more she tried to think about not falling, the more she was certain she would. So, she stayed mid-rope for a minute, looking down and then trying not to look down but not not looking down because how could you not look down?!!

"Everything all right up there, Cassie?" Mrs. Simmons called.

Why was she being spoken to? She was dangling from a rope, people! No one should be shouting at her. Of course, she looked down again — because it's rude not to at least try to make eye contact — and all she saw was Mary Ellen. She just stood there, staring up at Cassie, a mean grin on her face, her unmanicured hands on her hips.

What was Cassie supposed to respond, anyway? "No, it's really not okay up here at a trillion feet above sea level!" *The fact that I might fall and maim myself is not an issue at all.*

She settled on "Yes, just super!"

She took a deep, cleansing breath, flipped her red curls back, and started to pull herself up. She counted in French in her mind. This was the best and only thing she could do to stop herself from thinking about plummeting to an ungraceful crash on the plastic, sweaty, yellow vinyl gym mats beneath her.

She was feeling a little more confident by the time she pulled her way to the top. Her hands burned from the rope, her upper lip was dewy, but her hair, of course, was perfectly in place (at least she hoped it was!). When she got to the top, she slowly looked down. And what Cassie saw from the top of the gym ceiling surprised her. Everyone down there looked kind of normal. Cassie was sure that they were all feeling a little stupid having to climb ropes. And, most of them were just hanging out and talking. Some girls were even cheering their struggling ropemates on.

Suddenly, Cassie wished Etoile was in her gym class so she had someone to cheer *her* on. But even without her, from up there, nothing looked so bad. Even Mary Ellen had stopped her staring and was helping one of the Nightmare Sisters up onto the rope. Boys were goofing around and about to get into trouble. It was all sort of like her old school. Well, without all the girls that she loved. And with, like, zero hair spray. Or gloss. Or color. Oh, no, stop!

Before she let herself down, Cassie gave herself one second for a victory smile. She realized that she would NEVER be up there again, so she savored this life millisecond. Then she took a deep breath and happily let herself glide down the rope, her cobweb sweater perfectly fluttering in the breeze.

CHAPTER 10

I'm Sitting Right Here, Just Come and Sign Up, Already!

At lunch, Cassie and Etoile hung a sign advertising FASHION SHOW TEAM on the cafeteria table and held a clipboard with a sign-up sheet. Cassie kept her eyes on the crowd.

"Cass, you have to chill out!" Etoile said, taking a bite of a Rice Krispie treat. "People will sign up. I'm sure of it."

"It doesn't feel that way at all. I mean, we've already eaten our lunches. And unless we nibble at that Rice Krispie treat krispie by krispie, I just don't think we have that much time left." Cassie was tapping her nails on the table. She was trying her best to keep her spirits up, but this wasn't feeling so good. There were only eleven minutes left before the bell and *no one* had signed up yet. Even though it was mortifying, Cassie was relieved that PV helped to get the word out when she made her morning announcements after homeroom, telling everyone about the show. But she practically fainted when PV started going on about "the importance of new ideas" and once referred to Cassie as "our new Texan friend." It was twenty seconds of total eyes-to-the-ground embarrassment.

New Texan friend? People would actually have to be *my friend to say that.*

But Cassie had Etoile. And she knew she was lucky for that — to have someone sit next to her at the unpopular sign-up table. But the girls sat there in total silence, the seconds ticking by as they stared out into the crowd.

And then —

"There's Jonah!" Etoile said, jumping up. A boy was approaching their table. Cassie had seen him in the hallways but didn't know he and Etoile were friends. He was all freckles, with a big smile and a mess of sandy waves on his head.

"Jonah Thomas, this is Cassie Knight," Etoile said.

Cassie extended her hand toward Jonah. He met her hand with a good shake.

"Jonah, Cassie has just moved here from Texas

and she is in charge of the fashion show. And we need you to get your friends involved."

Jonah shrugged his shoulders. "What for?"

"Because we need your support. And because I said so," Etoile said, matter-of-factly.

"But I don't like fashion stuff," Jonah protested, shrugging again.

"I know. But we need people to do, like, all the other stuff — music, lights, the set."

"Do you like any of those things?" Cassie asked hopefully.

"Sorta," Jonah said, his hands in his pockets.

"Cassie, Jonah is the best artist! We need him to help. And *he* can get all of his friends to help," Etoile said.

Etoile was a girl on a mission!

"And, besides, I've known him forever and he has to do what I say. We're sort of like brother and sister — our mothers met in the hospital when we were born — isn't that amazing?"

"Totally!" Cassie said.

"Yeah," Jonah said, smiling suddenly, "she was, like, always crying and stuff. Such an annoying baby."

Etoile shoved him and they both laughed. "Okay, so sign up, right now," Etoile said.

Jonah took the pen off of the sign-up clipboard and wrote his name.

"Sign up some of the other boys, too. You know they'll do it if you tell them you are."

Obediently, Jonah wrote three other names down. "Okay? Can I go now?"

Cassie couldn't believe it. Four people! "Okay, the first meeting is tomorrow, after school," she said.

"And don't be late!" Etoile said.

Cassie laughed at how bossy she was with him. She didn't know Etoile had that side to her. "Thanks so much!"

Etoile was distracted by something, her eyes fixed straight ahead of her. "I think it worked."

Cassie turned to look. A trio of girls was headed directly toward the sign-up table. They were a grade older than Cassie and the closer they got, the harder her heart pounded in her chest.

But when they got to the table, they said four of the sweetest words Cassie had ever heard:

"Can we sign up?"

CHAPTER 11

Okay, Time Is Flying

Cassie didn't realize how quickly winter could go by, even when it snows so much. She had learned the art of not slipping on the ice and had even had a fun snowball fight with Etoile. Before she knew it, the plans for the Fash Bash Fashion Show (that was what she and Etoile had decided to call it, in a moment of pure inspiration) were coming together and there was even a hint of warmth in the Maine air. Cassie could not wait to bid *adieu* to the snow.

Things were moving along relatively smoothly. Cassie hadn't quite made legions of friends, but she couldn't worry about her social woes when there was so much work to do. Plus, she did have Etoile — and a motley group of volunteers. Some were secret fashion fans, some were just looking to add an extracurricular to their list, and some, well,

Cassie had no idea why they were there. And when Lynn Bauman — one half of Mary Ellen's Nightmare Sisters — signed up to help, Cassie almost fainted. Really. She didn't know what to do!

The Mary Ellen factor was a troubling one. She was automatically on the committee because of her involvement with the fund-raiser in the years before. But she never came to the meetings and she and Cassie didn't speak at all when they did see each other. Mary Ellen was doing an important job, working directly with the National Arbor Day Foundation. And Cassie was grateful that she was, so she could focus on the fashions.

Here's how everything was shaping up in Cassie's adorable Lisa Frank mini notebook:

✔Staff Assignments: All positions filled, including: Vice President of Polish, Secretary of Shadow, Treasurer of Gloss, VP of Blush, VP of Hair products, VP of Dresses, VP of Cute Shirts, VP of Pants, VP of Accessories. And so far so good, there is some style in Maine!! Etoile=VP of the Entire Show. Me=President and VP of Shoes. Totally!

✔Girl Models: 11 outfits. Totally and utterly complete and all divine and springtastic! Total faves: pink and pearl Junko Shimada cotton dress with cap sleeves and totally amazing belt;

the classic Lilly Pulitzer Carolee dress; the way hip L.A.M.B strap bow gown.

✓Boy Models: 9 outfits, 8 totally and utterly complete. From cute and casual to dressy and dashing. Just one more.

✓Hair products: done! Thanks to the fantastico Fabrizio. Texas in the house!

✓Accessories: in process, thanks to Lynn Nightmare's mother, who designs her own jewelry. Gorgeous corals and dangly pendants, glittery rings, and chunky necklaces.

✓Models' Makeup: deliciously bright and darling, shimmery and glittery! A frosty palette for a warm spring glow. And an artist from the mall makeup counter to help us on the night of the show! Can't wait to show those girls how to rock some gloss.

✓Polish: springy and flirty. About a zillion choices to choose from!

✓And, of course, shoes!! Just three pairs left to find.

✓Sets: bright and colorful. Being created under the guidance of Jonah, who is rocking it!

✓Music: The boys are tweaking and perfecting. All very sassy and poppy.

✓Teaching the models how to work the runway: yikes. Not as smooth as I was hoping. It's like they *all have a fashion-walk impairment. Etoile said they'll get it. I hope so!*

✓Invitations and banners: in progress. Wording is genius. To the printer on Friday! Will be spectacular!

✓Tickets: Being printed.

The Fash Bash Committee was really working hard. And Cassie's parents and Etoile's parents — along with PV, Mr. B, and Rose Miller, the friendly cafeteria lady — were making sure that all the stuff stayed organized and on schedule. And even Erin, far away in Houston, was advising on spring fashion combos with the help of Cassie's camera phone.

Of course Cassie's favorite part of all of this was going to the mall after school with the staff, splitting up, and asking for clothes and shoe donations. They even got a tailor who agreed to hem the clothes for everyone. And to top it off, a few stylists from a salon agreed to do hair for the show.

On the final excursion to the mall, in search of the last three pairs of shoes, Cassie and Etoile walked together, sipping Häagen-Dazs Sorbet Sippers. They felt they'd deserved a treat.

As they walked past the mirrored fountain wall, Cassie stopped to reapply her gloss and Etoile sprayed her hair with a small pump bottle.

"What's that?" Cassie asked, her pointer finger creating a perfect swoop across her lips.

"It's hair spray."

"That's *so* not hair spray." Cassie stuck her hand in her purse and pulled out a big aerosol can. "*This is* hair spray!" She popped off the top and coated her hair with a cloud of mist.

Etoile waved her hand in front of her face. "Ew! What is *that*?" She coughed dramatically.

"This is hair spray! Not that silly little stuff you use."

"Cass, c'mon! Do you really think the girl who is running Fundraising Fashion Show to Save the Planet should really be using an aerosol hair spray? It's *so* bad for the environment."

Cassie covered her mouth in shock. Etoile was right. *Of course.* How had she never once thought of that?

Etoile handed Cassie the bottle. Cassie took it and examined it. It looked cute, all flowers and blue sky. "Fresh Botanicals Mist?"

"Try it." Etoile smiled at her reassuringly.

"I don't know. The word *mist* scares me a little. Does it do anything?" Cassie pushed the bottle back toward Etoile.

"Cass!"

Nervously, Cassie handed her Sorbet Sipper to

Etoile and sprayed the right side of her hair with an easy pump. She scrunched, then moved to the next section. Soon, she was enveloped in a mist of yummy freshness.

She smiled cautiously. "And it will really hold?"

"Totally!" Etoile said. "Isn't it delicious?"

Cassie turned and gave Etoile a big hug. "Thank you so much!"

Thrilled with her fresh-smelling hair, she gave her lips one more check before the two girls walked to the final frontier: the only shoe store they hadn't checked out.

"Okay," Cassie said to Etoile, "this is it. Keep your fingers crossed."

They walked in together and admired strappy little sandals, the most precious pair of espadrilles, and delicious green pumps.

"Hi, can I help you?" a very sweet-looking young woman asked Cassie. She wore a khaki hunting jacket with a starched white shirt underneath, perfectly worn-in jeans, and truly genius leopard-print flats. Her hair was pin-straight and luxuriously brown, with one thick blond highlight. Cassie thought she was probably in college.

"Hi, I'm Cassie." Cassie extended her hand and they shook. "And this is Etoile." Etoile gave a handshake as well. "We are both on the committee of Oak Grove's charity fashion show."

"Cool," the salesgirl said.

"We've been asking stores in the mall if they would donate some things for it. All of the proceeds are going to buy saplings for the communities in the country that need them the most," Cassie recited proudly.

"That's so great," the girl said. "So, do you guys have your eye on some shoes here for the show?"

"Yes," Cassie said.

The girl scanned the row of shoes in front of them. "Can I guess which you like?"

Oh, the Shoe Game! Cassie loved the Shoe Game! "Of course."

The salesgirl didn't hesitate for a moment. "You're doing spring, right? No need to let winter last any longer than it has to. Especially here in Maine," she said with an eye roll. She went directly for the espadrilles. "These."

Cassie nodded in total and complete agreement.

"Are all the clothes colorful and bright?" the girl asked.

"Yes," Etoile said, dazzled and delighted.

"Well, then, these are perfect." Cassie knew where she was headed. Uh-huh — to the strappy sandals. Each strap was a different bright color. So cute!

"You're a shoe psychic!" Etoile said. They all giggled.

"So, the last pair . . ." The girl looked around the store, deep in thought. Cassie felt relieved and excited all at once. This was really the last big thing to cross off the list.

"The last pair have to be these," she said, holding up a pair of spring-green pumps.

"How did you know all of this?" Etoile asked.

"You just know sometimes," she said, smiling. "Let me talk to the owner and I'll get these for your show." As she walked to the back, Cassie sat down and pulled out her notebook.

✔Shoes – done!!

CHAPTER 12

Does it Really Snow in April?

You are Cordially Invited
to The Fash Bash
a Celebration of the Fashions of Spring

Saturday, April 14
8 P.M.
The Runway at the Oak Grove Gym
Tickets: $5 at the door

All proceeds will be donated to the
National Arbor Day Foundation.

It was the day before the big show and Cassie could feel the excitement in the air. Even though she still wasn't the biggest hit at Oak Grove, Cassie knew some people were looking forward to it. Especially the people on the Fash Bash Committee. But there was one person who clearly wasn't excited: Mary Ellen.

As she walked down the hallway, Cassie smiled at all of the signs Jonah and the boys had created. She was totally impressed with their work. The signs were all different colors, but Cassie insisted on one thing: teal in each one. (Of course!)

She was still waiting on Etoile's final answer about the jacket, but she knew it was going to be a yes. She could feel it.

She headed to the gym. The run-through was in just a few minutes. Jonah had told her that the set had the finishing touches on it and she was dying to see it.

As she opened the door to the gym, she gasped in utter amazement. The boy committee had created a stage and runway that would have any designer in Paris panting. The runway itself was painted a shiny deep blue, and a clean white screen hung at the back. Cassie wanted the backstage area to be the actual backdrop to the show, so the audience would be able to see everyone's shadows through the screen. The podium — and the mic! — were covered in marabou and crystals. It was all totally wonderful and gorgeous. Cassie wasn't surprised. She had even gotten her dad to help build the set on the weekends — and she knew what Paul could do.

Cassie wished Erin and the girls could come to see it all. She pulled out her camera phone and snapped a pic of the set to send to them.

Just then Mary Ellen walked in. Mary Ellen had freaked when she heard Lynn was on the Committee. They were still on speaking terms, but Lynn was not one of the favorites like she used to be.

Mary Ellen walked calmly across the gym. "So, this is it?" she asked Cassie, her words echoing.

"Yeah. It's looking so great," Cassie answered cautiously.

"Well, everything is all set with the Arbor Day Foundation. Principal Veronica just finished up a phone call with them. And we will send them *whatever* money the show makes next week." Mary Ellen made it sound like the show wasn't going to make any money.

Cassie wouldn't allow Mary Ellen to get in the way of her excitement. "That's fantastic. Thanks so much for all that you've done." She smiled and turned away then, excited to go backstage and see everything. Even the hair and makeup people were coming to the run-through today.

As Cassie stepped onto the runway, Mary Ellen said, "So, I guess you're not nervous about that huge snowstorm that's on its way?"

Cassie stopped, almost tripping but catching herself. *"What?"* How could it snow in April?

"They're calling for almost two feet." Mary Ellen had a look of sheer happiness on her face. "Good luck with the dress rehearsal." She turned dramatically, her frumpy tartan skirt twirling, and walked to the door — with a smile on her face, Cassie was sure.

Does it really snow in April?

There was no time to think about it now, because the Fash Bash staff was arriving. Cassie had to get them ready for tomorrow, snow or no, and she had to make sure they all knew how to work it down the runway. She'd shown them a thing or two and even assigned them to watch as much fashion show coverage on the Style Network as they possibly could, but she still wasn't sure they were ready. At the last rehearsal, one of the boys actually *fell off* the runway.

"Okay, guys, while we wait for hair and makeup to come, I thought we could practice our runway one last time." Cassie waited for a negative response but was surprised when they lined up. She looked at Etoile, shocked.

"All right," Etoile said, "Jonah, can you give us some music?"

"Sure," he called from backstage. In a moment, the gym was filled with a lively *thump-thump-thump.* Cassie sat back and watched as the models strutted down the runway. They'd been practicing! Each one had their own style, their own method of working the perfect sashay.

Cassie squealed with joy and grabbed Etoile's hand. "They're unbelievable!" she said.

"I told you they'd get it!" Etoile said.

They were both super-wowed by Lynn, who worked the runway better than any supermodel could hope to. She was the perfect combination of confidence and nerves, and her long legs cut perfect, sharp angles. Maybe it was time to give up on her nickname. No Nightmare could ever be so beautiful!

CHAPTER 13

Yup, That's Right, It Snows in April

The day of the show had arrived. Cassie opened her eyes and took a sec to admire her room. The Fash Bash was so time consuming but she really was so proud of how her room had come together. Two of the walls were a gorgeous teal, and the others were a warm, wonderful white. It totally made her feel like a robin in the nest, and she adored it. Her new bedding was really different from the way it was in Houston. There, she had pink island patchwork. But here in Maine, she wanted something more snuggly and cozy. She and Sheila opted for an amazing chocolate brown duvet and bright white sheets.

Divinity.

The rest of the room felt familiar and she was glad for some normality. She had her wooden vanity, with the stain on top from when she spilled nail polish remover on it; her tall dresser with the lattice doors; and her white desk and her big, fuzzy blue rug. That rug ruled. Just the perfect balance of soft and scratchy on bare feet.

She sprang out of bed with a satisfied sigh, slid on her marabous, and marched to the window. Snow or no?

Of course, Mary Ellen had been right. The ground, the trees, everything was covered in snow!

Cassie looked out the window at the snow falling. She had to admit it: It was beautiful. Sure, its effect on her shoe collection was unforgivable. Cassie had ruined almost every pair of shoes she adored, from her chunky Steve Maddens to her Kitson Lovebird sneaks. She had finally decided, after much thought and deliberation with Erin, to get a pair of duck boots. It was a super-difficult decision to make but she had to do it, for the preservation of her beautiful shoes. (And Cassie was no fool — she changed out of her duck boots the moment she got to school.)

Cassie and staff were due to report to Oak Grove by two P.M. There was a ton of hair and makeup and last-minute stuff to deal with. And snow!

She had her whole morning planned, starting with a peaceful breakfast with Paul and Sheila.

"So, the snow's not going to stop people from coming to the show, right?" she asked over a bowl of oatmeal.

"It's not, I promise you," Paul said. "Do you think that this is the first time these people have seen a snowstorm in April? They're used to it. And they all have the big cars to prove it!"

"And, I spoke to Etoile's mom this morning and they're ready to go," Sheila added. "She said nothing could stop them from getting there!"

Etoile still hadn't said a word about the jacket, and Cassie was nervous. Of course, there was a Plan B for the jacket but she didn't want to go with Plan B. When she finished eating, she went upstairs to call Etoile. She didn't want to put pressure on her, but her curiosity was getting the best of her. She grabbed her cell phone and saw that she had two new messages.

First, from Erin

You get 'em, girl! xox, Erin and the girls

Oh, what would she do without her Texas support team?

She clicked to the next message.

1 new picture mail.

Cassie loved picture mail. And she couldn't wait to see who it was from! She waited as the picture loaded. And then, finally, when the picture came up on her screen, Cassie squealed with delight: a fabulous, handmade, Etoile original jacket! Cassie couldn't believe it.

She dialed Etoile's number as quickly as she could.

The phone buzzed for a second before Etoile picked up. "What do you think?" she asked, a slight note of panic in her voice.

"I think you are a genius," Cassie said.

"Really? Are you sure?"

"I can't wait to see it in person!"

"I am totally nervous to show it."

"Don't be," Cassie said. "It will be fabulous and so will you, Miss Emcee."

Cassie wanted to be backstage, making sure everything was running smoothly. And she knew Etoile would do a terrific job up there.

"Okay, don't remind me!"

"I can't believe it's snowing, though," Cassie said, peeking out the window at the falling flakes.

"Why? I didn't really even think about it."

"Mary Ellen made it seem like it would be the end of the fashion show if it snowed."

"Cassie, come on, you're too smart to be that

gullible. It always snows like this in the spring. And look at it this way; it's even cooler to have a spring fashion show in the middle of a snowstorm!"

Cassie hadn't thought of it that way.

"You're right. You are SO right." Cassie looked at the time. "And there's only three hours till we have to be there!"

When she hung up, Cassie took her new yummy teal dress from her closet and laid it out on her bed. She'd decided to wear something lovely but functional, and this dress was it. It was light and flowy, with thick beaded straps, a fab flower right in the center, and silvery beading at the hem. It was dreamy. AND comfortable. She pulled her shoes out of the closet—and, of course, her duck boots.

Duck boots to a fashion show? She was *so* Maine!

CHAPTER 14

It's Fashion Time, People! Fashion Time!

Backstage was madness! It was really dark except for the hair and makeup room. There were clothes *everywhere,* and the sweet smell of natural mist hair spray wafted through every now and then. Half of the girls were getting their makeup done and the others were getting worked on by a hair stylist. Cassie made it a point to visit with everyone and see how they were doing. She had her camera phone in hand, so she could instantly document all of their beauty.

Then she stood behind Etoile, who was getting her brown tresses smoothed and flattened. Total roar! Her poker-straight hair fell perfectly around her face, making her brown eyes glow.

"You are gorgeous!" Cassie said, while the stylist did her thing.

"Thanks! I can't believe we're finally here! I can't

believe you pulled this off!" Etoile beamed from the chair.

"What I can't believe is how perfect this jacket is! You are brilliant!" Cassie stepped closer to the jacket hanging on the rack. It was the perfect combination of elegant and hip, with its denim jacket cut and its opulent sequin details. *Wow.*

"Thanks so much for making me do it. All of this is just so great!" Etoile beamed.

Cassie walked to the front of the chair and flung her arms around Etoile.

"All right, all right, enough, you two! There's work to do!" PV said as she walked into the room.

Cassie gasped. PV looked incredible. Her hair was out of the bun and curled just so. And instead of one of her sad suits, she wore a pink tweed blazer and matching skirt and heels. Heels on PV! And lipstick!

Cassie was stunned. "Look at you."

PV stopped and smiled. "You know, I like to dress up sometimes, too."

"Give us a twirl," Cassie said, spinning her index finger.

"No! Girls! No!" PV tried — in vain — to sound firm. She was blushing.

Etoile popped out of her chair. "Oh, please, Principal Veronica!"

And with that, PV gave the best, proudest outfit twirl in the History of Outfit Twirls. Cassie and Etoile applauded.

Just then, Mr. B came gliding into the room in a gray Calvin Klein suit. He had bought it himself and he just looked too debonair for words.

"Can I come in?" he asked.

"Of course, Robert," PV said.

"So, are you guys ready?" he asked, his smile toothy and happy.

Etoile and Cassie looked at each other. "We are totally ready!" Cassie said.

"Before we start," PV said, getting serious, "I want to thank you, Cassie, for your wonderful spirit. It's been a long time since we've had a student like you here at Oak Grove."

"Thank you so much," Cassie said, tears filling her eyes. Etoile grabbed her hand and squeezed tight.

Jonah came running through backstage just then. He looked perfectly arty in his black pants, black Converse, black button-down, and skinny red tie.

"Cassie, six minutes to showtime!" He stopped and put a headset on her so they could communicate throughout the show. Cassie loved wearing it. She felt like a pop star on her world tour!

Just before the show started, Cassie had

everyone stand in a circle and hold hands. PV and Mr. B were there; Paul and Sheila; Etoile's mom; Rose Miller; and all the parents who had helped. It was pep talk time.

"Okay, you gorgeous and glamorous people: The only thing left for all of you to do is to rock that runway and have some fun." She looked out at the circle of people and was so impressed by them. They all looked back at her with excitement in their eyes.

"Good luck out there. Break a leg. And thank you so much for all that you've done. This is just the best!"

"Two minutes till curtain!" Jonah said over the headset.

It was time.

"Okay, guys, places!" Cassie shouted, her heart pounding.

Cassie gave Etoile a giant hug. "Good luck!" she said.

"Wait! I have something for you," Etoile said, reaching into her purse. She extracted a simple silver necklace with a tiny star pendant on it. "My name might mean "star," but you really *are* one, Cassie."

Tears ran down Cassie's cheeks as Etoile put the necklace on her. "I am so proud to be your friend."

That was one of the nicest things that anyone had ever said to Cassie. Thank goodness for waterproof mascara!

"One minute, Cassie!" Jonah said.

They hugged again and Etoile ran off to the other side of the stage, ready to take the podium.

Cassie turned on her mic so Jonah could hear her. "Okay, Jonah, let's make some fashion history." She nodded at PV and Mr. B, who were going to do a very brief welcome. She pulled her turquoise bangle up on her arm.

"Houselights down," she said. She peered at the packed (*packed!*) auditorium from backstage. The lights went out and a hush fell over the room.

"Cue spotlights."

The lights went up and PV and Mr. Blackwell walked out. As they greeted everyone, Cassie did a last review of all the models.

Once she heard PV wrap up her intro, Cassie clicked her headset back into the "talk" position. "Lights out." She waited a few beats. "Spotlight up on the podium." She gave Etoile a thumbs-up from across the stage, and Etoile walked out onto the stage.

"Ladies and gentlemen, welcome to Oak Grove's Charity Spring Fashion Show, or as we like to call it, the Fash Bash. Thank you all for coming to this important event. . . ."

Cassie walked the line of models, straightening a lapel, fixing a strand or two of hair, and running the lint brush over a few people.

When she heard Etoile say "Let's begin," Cassie ran to the edge of the screen.

"Here we go," Jonah said in Cassie's headset.

"Roger that. Cue music."

The music pumped out over the sound system.

"Stage lights down and swirling spotlights up."

The stage went dark for a moment and then bright pink, blue, and green lights popped up and swirled across the catwalk.

Cassie took the first model's hand, gave her a big smile, and mouthed, "Go."

Obediently, she strutted past the screen and onto the runway.

Etoile picked up right on cue. "This stunning Malicious Designs lace and cotton dress is not to be believed. It features an ultra-fab cut and a soothing, springy cream color that provides the epitome of chic."

Cassie watched from backstage. *Good pivot, good smile, and some fierce attitude.*

"Next up, we have a Betsy Johnson double silk stretch set. With its pleated skirt and wrap top, the dazzling pink lines will have you ready for anything this spring!"

Etoile handled it very well when her jacket hit the runway. She and Cassie had written the description together and decided that they would say it was created by "Star Designs." And it got quite a reaction from the audience, worn with a fitted pair of Ralph Lauren boy shorts. Cassie was so excited for Etoile. She was going to make sure to tell the school newspaper that Etoile had designed it.

Model after model, each was perfectly poised, smiling, and stunning. Cassie was so excited and so focused on the timing that she was shocked when they got to Lynn, the last model of the show. Lynn was rocking her L.A.M.B. Strap Bow Gown. She was a vision on the runway. As Cassie peered from the sideline, she saw Mary Ellen in the audience. She was sitting with Deirdre Nightmare and some of her other cronies, looking happier and more excited than Cassie had ever seen her.

Once Lynn made it backstage, Cassie sent all of the models out for a final bow. As they filed out, laughing and smiling, Etoile spoke into the mic.

"Before we end," Etoile said, "I would like to introduce you all to the star of this show. She said she wasn't going to come out on the stage, but I think we can get her out. . . . Ladies and gentlemen, put your hands together for the toast of Oak Grove, President of the Fash Bash Committee and VP of Shoes!"

Cassie was frozen.

The audience applauded and everyone backstage joined in.

Okay. I have no choice. I have to do this.

Etoile continued, "I present to you Miss Cassie Cyan Knight!"

Cassie took a step through the curtains, the bright spotlight hitting her in the face.

She paused for a second, and the audience went wild. Etoile and the models clapped like crazy.

"You get 'em," Jonah said on her headset.

Cassie's smile grew larger and larger. She walked to Etoile and grabbed her hand. Together, they walked down the runway. And when it was Cassie's turn to take center stage, she put her hands on her hips, laughing.

And created a brand-new Life Rule.

Life Rule #58: You can do anything you want to do. No matter what you might think is in the way.

A cheer came from the audience and Cassie

waved. She grabbed Etoile's hand again and they bowed.

"How are we ever going to top this?" Etoile said over the noise.

Cassie squeezed their hands tight. "Oh, I have an idea or two."

The girls turned together then and walked the length of the runway.

As they bowed with the models, PV hurried to the podium. "Ladies and gentlemen, I want to let you know that because of all of the hard work — and your support — we have raised more money than we ever have in the history of the Oak Grove fund-raiser!"

Cassie was stunned. Incredible!

"And it is because of the dedication of one young woman," PV continued, "that all of this was possible. Please, let's give her another round of applause. . . . Miss Cassie Knight."

The audience applauded like mad and soon they were chanting, "Cassie! Cassie!" Cassie was overwhelmed. She never thought it would happen like this. She looked out at the crowd and bowed, grateful, once again, for waterproof mascara.

Paul walked to the foot of the stage and handed Cassie an enormous bouquet of roses. "We're so proud of you, Cass," he said, as she leaned down to take them from him.

Everyone on the catwalk applauded and shouted before they ran backstage. In the midst of a flurry of hugs and congratulations, Cassie saw Mary Ellen talking to Lynn. Mary Ellen looked nice, in a Laura Ashley-ish flowered dress and a matching headband. She would have been a perfect model for the show, with those long legs and perfect skin. Cassie hesitated for a moment and then decided to go and say hello.

"Hey, Lynn!" Cassie said. "You were gorgeous out there! That dress was made for you."

Lynn blushed. "Thanks so much. And thank you for letting me help. I had so much fun." She caught herself and looked at Mary Ellen nervously.

"Thanks for coming," Cassie said, courageously, to Mary Ellen.

"I came because Lynn was in the show." Mary Ellen didn't make eye contact.

"Well, we couldn't have done it without her and her hard work," Cassie said, proud of Lynn for standing up to Mary Ellen.

Cassie was about to turn away, but before she did, she said to Mary Ellen "I really like your dress. The colors are pretty."

It looked like she was trying to fight it, but Mary

Ellen's face brightened up into a smile. "Thanks." Her cheeks flushed. "It was really a good show. And thank you for raising so much money. I don't know how you did it."

"How *we* did it. We did it together!"

"Thanks," Mary Ellen said, this time sincerely.

Hmm, Cassie thought, *there is hope for her!*

She wanted to say something else, wanted to tell Mary Ellen to lighten up and maybe try some lip gloss and not judge people right away. But, instead, she took a deep breath. *Not yet*, she thought. "Thanks again for all of your help," she said. She gave Lynn a quick hug and walked toward another group of people.

Just then, her phone buzzed in her purse, and she flipped the phone open. It was a text from Erin, of course.

So?? Are we smiling??

Cassie turned around and saw all of the Fash Bash Committee standing together, laughing and talking, still floating on clouds. How could she be more lucky? Her best friend from Houston was texting her, and her new friends in Maine were all standing around her, celebrating their first success together. Cassie's heart swelled. She had so many terrific people in her life. And they loved Cassie for being *Cassie*.

She texted back:

We are more than smiling! We are happy! xo

And with that, she flipped her phone closed, scrunched her hair, and sashayed over to the group.

check out

THE Accidental CHEERLEADER

by Mimi McCoy

Another

Candy Apple book . . .

just for you.

CHAPTER Two

Sophie leaned against her locker and checked her watch for the third time that morning. Eight-fifteen. Kylie was late.

The hall was starting to fill with students. Noise echoed through the corridor as they hollered greetings, excited to see one another after the summer. A few kids Sophie knew said hi as they passed her. They all were wearing bright clothes in the latest fashions. They sported new haircuts and dark tans, and the ones who'd gotten their braces off flashed extra-wide pearly white smiles.

The first day of the school year wasn't really like school at all, Sophie thought. It was more like a commercial for school. All the kids wore cool clothes and looked happy, the teachers acted nice, and the classes actually seemed interesting. It was like watching a movie preview that turns out to be way better than the movie itself.

As she waited for Kylie, Sophie eyed her own lime green corduroys. She wished she'd worn something else. The pants were too heavy for the warm late-summer morning. But she'd promised Kylie she wouldn't wear the dragon jeans, and these were her only other new pants.

"Sophie!"

Kylie rushed up, her blond curls bouncing like hair in a shampoo commercial. She threw her arms around Sophie as if they hadn't seen each other in years, even though they'd talked on the phone just the night before.

"Sorry I'm late," Kylie said breathlessly. "I missed the bus, so my mom had to drive, but she couldn't find the car keys. Boy, was she mad —"

She broke off when she saw Sophie staring at her. "What?" Kylie asked.

"Your jeans," Sophie said.

"What?" Kylie looked at her legs. "Did I spill something on them? What is it? Toothpaste?" She craned her neck, looking for stains.

"You wore *the* jeans," Sophie said, eyeing the red-and-gold dragon on Kylie's left leg. "Kye, we agreed that *neither* of us would wear those on the first day of school. Remember?"

Kylie's eyes opened so wide Sophie could see white all around her irises. "Ooooops! I totally forgot, Soph. I was running late, and my mom was yelling at me to hurry. So I grabbed the first thing —"

"Whatever. Forget it," Sophie said, cutting her off. *It's just like Kylie to forget her own rule,* she thought.

"Really, Soph, I forgot. You aren't mad, are you? They're just jeans."

"Right," said Sophie.

The thing was, Sophie knew Kylie hadn't meant to break her rule. She sometimes did things without thinking. Sophie knew that. She was used to it.

So why did she feel so annoyed?

She tried to shrug off the feeling. Sophie didn't like to make a big deal out of things. "So, what do you think of my locker?" she asked, changing the subject.

Her locker was in the sunny southeast corridor on the second floor. Normally, seventh-graders were assigned lockers on the lower floors. But this year their class was bigger than usual, so some of them had been given lockers in the upstairs hallways, near the eighth-graders.

"You're lucky you got a good one," said Kylie.

"Mine's across from the cafeteria. The whole hallway smells like barfburgers." Barfburgers was what Kylie called school food, whether it was a burger or not. She claimed it was all made from the same mystery substance, and it all made you want to barf.

"Yeah, it's nice up here," Sophie agreed, looking around.

Kylie suddenly gasped. "And I just saw something that makes it a whole lot nicer! Scott sighting, dead ahead."

Sophie turned. Across the hallway, Scott Hersh was leaning casually against a row of lockers, talking to a friend. As they watched, he turned and put his bag inside the locker directly across from Sophie's.

"I cannot believe your locker is right across from Scott Hersh's!" Kylie's whisper was so loud, Sophie was sure Scott could hear it on the other side of the hallway. "You are the luckiest girl alive."

"I guess."

Sophie didn't get why everyone was so into Scott. He was good-looking, she supposed. He had deep brown eyes and a scar above his lip that gave him a cute, crooked smile. But Sophie thought he seemed aloof and unfriendly. He didn't talk much, and when he did it was only with other football players.

"Trade lockers with me," Kylie pleaded.

"Nope," said Sophie.

"I'll be your best friend."

It was an old joke between them. They had already been best friends for almost as long as either of them could remember. "You wouldn't send your best friend down to barfburger hall, would you?" asked Sophie.

Kylie sighed. "You're right. I could never do that to you. I guess it just means I'm going to be here *all the time*."

"Fine with me."

Just then, there was a ripple in the flow of hallway movement. Several kids turned to look as a quartet of girls strode down the center of the corridor.

In the lead was a petite girl with almond-shaped eyes and long wavy black hair that reached halfway down her back. Everyone in school knew Keisha Reyes. She was head of the cheerleading team and the most popular girl at Meridian. The red-haired girl to her right, walking so close that she matched Keisha's steps, was her best friend, Courtney Knox. Following on their heels were two blonde girls — Amie and Marie Gildencrest, the only identical twins at Meridian Middle School. Courtney, Amie, and Marie were all cheerleaders, too.

As they walked down the hall, the girls shouted greetings to the other popular eighth-graders. Keisha had a perfect smile, Sophie noticed. It was wide and full of even, white teeth. Courtney, on the other hand, looked like she was pouting even when she wasn't. Sophie thought it was because of all the lip gloss she wore.

"Heeeey, Scott!" Keisha called flirtatiously as she passed.

Scott flashed his crooked grin and waved at her.

Someone called Sophie's and Kylie's names. A boy's voice. Confused, Sophie pulled her gaze from the cheerleaders and looked around. There was Joel Leo making his way toward them through the crowded hallway.

Joel had moved in down the street from Kylie the year before, at the beginning of sixth grade. They had become friends riding the bus together. Sophie had gotten to know him a little, too, when she took the bus home with Kylie after school.

"Joel-e-o!" Kylie exclaimed.

"Hey, Joel," said Sophie.

"What's up, guys?" he said. "How was your summer?"

"Oh, you know, the usual," Kylie answered, with a bored wave of her hand. "Jetting to Hollywood. Shopping in London. Sunbathing in Saint Trapeze."

Joel smiled. "You mean Saint-Tropez?"

"Yeah, there, too," Kylie said.

Joel and Sophie laughed. "We mostly hung out at the pool," Sophie told him. "What about you?"

"Yeah, I didn't see you around," Kylie added.

"I was in California helping out on my aunt and uncle's farm," Joel told them. "They grow organic kiwis. Weird, huh?"

"Weird," Sophie agreed. "But it sounds kind of cool, too."

"It was pretty cool. They paid me six dollars an hour to pick fruit, and I got to eat all the kiwis I wanted. I don't really like them, though. Kiwis, I mean. They're all furry."

"Gross!" Kylie said. "So you spent the summer eating furry fruit? Sounds like a blast."

Joel smiled. "Naw, most of my family lives around there, too. I have some cousins who are pretty cool. They taught me how to surf."

The way he said "surf" gave Sophie a little chill. She tried to imagine Joel eating tropical fruit and surfing in southern California. It seemed incredibly exotic compared to hanging out by the pool.

Sophie always found Joel slightly mysterious. He didn't look like most of the other boys at Meridian. His hair was long and a little shaggy, and he wore T-shirts for bands that Sophie had never heard of. Even his name was unusual. Joel Leo. If you took off the *J* it was the same spelled forward and backward.

Sophie noticed how his teeth stood out white against his brown face. *He got tan over the summer,* she thought. *He looks good. In fact, he's cute. Way cute.*

As quickly as the thought came, Sophie pushed it away. Kylie and Joel were neighbors, and their parents were friends. She knew their families sometimes had dinner together, which in Sophie's mind practically made them related. If Kylie found out she had a crush on Joel, she'd never hear the end of it.

The bell for first period rang loudly, startling Sophie out of her thoughts.

"Well, I better go," Joel said. "I'll see you guys later." His eyes rested on Sophie for a moment. She felt the beginnings of a blush creep into her cheeks.

"Later, Joeleo," Kylie said cheerfully.

"Bye," Sophie murmured.

"Hey, by the way, Kylie," Joel said as he walked away, "cool pants!"

Kylie beamed. Sophie gritted her teeth, hating her lime green cords.

Later that day, Sophie stretched her legs across the seat in the last row of the bus. She worked the flavor out of a piece of cinnamon gum.

Kylie was sprawled out on the seat in front of Sophie, and Joel lounged in the seat across the aisle.

"I heard Keisha was dating a high-school guy over the summer," Kylie reported.

Kylie had spent the last fifteen minutes reviewing the summer gossip she'd picked up at school. Most of it centered around Keisha Reyes.

"I'm tired of hearing about Keisha Reyes. She's a snob," said Joel.

"Maybe people just *think* she's a snob because she's a cheerleader and she's pretty and popular. Maybe she's actually really nice. She has nice hair," Kylie pointed out.

"That's great logic, Kylie," Joel said. "Just because someone has nice hair doesn't mean she's a nice person."

Sophie sighed and let her attention drift. She wondered what it would be like to have a guy beg you to get back together. The crying part sounded awful, she decided. But it still would be nice to have a guy like you so much he called every night.

"Anyway," Kylie was saying, "I guess we'll know what they're all like pretty soon. We're probably going to be spending a lot of time with them."

"Spending a lot of time with whom?" Sophie asked. "What are you talking about?"

"Keisha and the other cheerleaders," Kylie told her. "Tryouts for the team are next week. I think we have a shot at making it."

"You're trying out for cheerleading?" Sophie was surprised. Kylie hadn't mentioned it before.

Kylie's smile could have lit up a football stadium. "Nope. *We're* trying out. I signed you up, too!"

There was a squeal of brakes as the bus lurched to a halt at Joel and Kylie's stop. Sophie sat bolt upright and stared over the seat back at her friend. "You did *what*?"

check out

THE BOY NEXT DOOR

by Laura Dower

Another

Candy Apple book . . .

just for you.

CHAPTER 1

✿✿✿ TARYN ✿✿✿

I Guess It's a Boy Thing

"Jeff Rasmussen, I'm going to get you for this!" I scream at the top of my lungs.

My head pounds and I reach up to make sure there's no bump. Meanwhile, Jeff zips across my lawn into his own backyard, taunting me the whole time.

"You can run," I scream even louder, "but you can't hide!"

I can't believe Jeff would do this. Sure, he's been teasing me for eleven summers straight. There have been times over the years when he's even dared to pinch or poke me, but he usually keeps his distance. And he never actually *hit* me with anything before, especially not a flying object.

Mostly he just calls me obnoxious names like "stinky" and "bones. " He sure knows how to make me squirm, the rat.

Of course, I've plotted my own kind of revenge. It drives Jeff crazy when I tease him right back about the two extra-long toes on his left foot. And I got him once with a mean triple-knuckled noogie. The main difference between my teasing and his, however, are the aftershocks.

A single harsh word from Jeff and I'm bawling for five minutes.

But Jeff's different. He never ever cries. He just laughs out loud.

I guess it's a boy thing.

Jeff's family and my family have been friends forever. His mom and my mom always remind us that Jeff and I were born on the exact same weekend at the same hospital in Rochester, New York. We both weighed exactly seven pounds and four ounces, and measured twenty inches. Sometimes I wonder if Jeff is actually my secret twin brother, except that I don't really need (or want) another brother. I already have three of those: Tim, Tom, and Todd. Three Taylor brothers is more than enough for anyone.

I guess the worst part about Jeff's sneak attack today was that he didn't hit me with a Wiffle ball or anything accidental. No, he hit me with a sneaker aimed directly at my head — a smelly, brown, disgusting sneaker with a rubber sole that's peeling off.

How gross is that?

"Jeff, where are you?" I growl, climbing over the break in the fence between our houses. I scramble through the thicket, trying hard not to scratch up my legs. I'm already covered from head to toe with mosquito bites.

It's too warm out today. The air feels like mashed potatoes and I can't find Jeff anywhere. He's not in the small shed behind his house. He's not under his front porch. I've checked all of his usual hiding spots.

I'm getting thirsty.

"Jeff, come out!" I cry. "Come on, it's too hot. Truce? Please?"

Jeff appears from around the side of his blue-shingled house. He's whistling and carrying two Popsicles. I take a cherry one. He keeps the lime. We sit on the porch steps. I realize that he's still only wearing one sneaker, the one he didn't hurl at my head.

"That really, really hurt, you know," I grumble, biting the end of my Popsicle.

He looks right through me. "Yeah, sorry, Taryn," he says. I want to believe him, but he's smirking.

"You're sorry?" I repeat, my eyes widening.

"Yeah, sorry. Truly."

"You mean it?" I ask, twisting the ends of my long, brown hair.

"Yeah," Jeff replies. "I didn't really mean to hit you. I just got carried away. And I know how gross my sneakers are."

He sounds genuine this time. As if.

But somehow, despite all the teasing over the years, Jeff always finds the right thing to say or do to make things better. Somehow, a word or even just a smile is like a Band-Aid, and I can instantly forgive Jeff for whatever he's done.

That's how it works with best friends.